The Smallest Monster
in the World

Also by William MacKellar

The Smallest Monster
in the World

by WILLIAM MacKELLAR

illustrated by Ursula Koering

DAVID McKAY COMPANY, Inc. NEW YORK

The Smallest Monster in the World

MANUFACTURED IN THE UNITED STATES OF AMERICA

VAN REES PRESS • NEW YORK

Typography by Charles M. Todd

To Phyllis A. Whitney
who has given so much to so many

The Smallest Monster
in the World

CHAPTER ONE

WULLIE leaned forward and stared, his heart beating just a little too fast. Had he been mistaken? Or had something just moved out in Loch Moyne? A long sinister blackness that had suddenly shattered the sparkling surface of the lake, it had vanished as quickly as it had come. *If* it had come. There was nothing there now. Only a seemingly endless sweep of wind-riffled water like dull frosted glass.

"Fiona"—the boy began, then stopped, sensing the slight tremor in his voice. The girl with the green eyes and red hair would merely laugh at him. Fiona was not only his sister, she was his older sister. Ten years older to be exact. And Fiona was exact about

1

everything. It all came from reading so many books. She looked up wearily now from the one she held in her lap and frowned slightly at the eight-year-old boy beside her.

"Yes, Wullie?" she asked patiently. "What is it this time?"

He gave a small cough, just to test the timbre of his voice. It seemed to be its old high pitched self again. He thrust a finger in the direction of Loch Moyne. "Just now, Fiona! About a hundred yards from the shore I am certain sure that something moved. I saw it!"

"Saw what, Wullie?"

"A—a—" he hesitated, afraid to dislodge the fearsome word from the tip of his tongue. It must have been perched right on the edge, though, for it fell off before he could do anything about it. "A monster."

Fiona closed her eyes, sighed, then shook her head. "Wullie Watson, are you never going to stop dreaming? In a few more weeks you'll be nine years old. It's time you stopped having all these fantasies. A monster, no less! You know full well there's no monster in Loch Moyne."

"Aye, but fine I know there's one over in Loch Ness," the boy returned stubbornly. "Everybody's heard about the Loch Ness Monster. It's been in all the papers. It's got a long neck and a long tail with a lot of humps in between. So if they've got a monster in Loch Ness, why now couldn't we have one here in Loch Moyne?"

Fiona closed her book. She pursed her lips as she collected her thoughts. "It's true that some people *think* there may be some strange creature in Loch Ness. Only no one, Wullie, knows for sure just what it is. If it's anything, which I strongly doubt."

"It's a monster," Wullie said doggedly. For someone as old as Fiona and who read as many books as she did, there was an awful lot of things she didn't seem to know.

"No one has proved there's a monster in Loch Ness, Wullie."

"Aye, but no one has proved there's not." He screwed his round freckled face into a frown as he looked down again at the water sparkling in the distance. "Anyway, I know I saw something just now, Fiona. It was dark and scaly. Must have been at least fifty feet long, I'm thinking."

She said, "Humph," more to herself than to her small brother before picking up her book again. "Everyone says you dream too much, Wullie."

He stared moodily off into the distance. Nothing stirred in Loch Moyne. Nothing stirred in the dour, lumpy hills. Nothing stirred in the great emptiness

3

of the sky. Nothing stirred anywhere. Surely in all of Scotland there was nowhere a scene of such desolation and emptiness. He grunted. "Och now, Fiona, and what else will there be to do around here than dream? Nothing ever happens around Loch Moyne and Abermuir. Aye, and if it did everybody would be too busy sleeping to see it."

The girl looked up, a new light in her green eyes. "Oh, I don't think it's quite that bad, Wullie. If Abermuir was as sleepy as all that, why would visitors come to our village for their holidays? People like that Professor Grant, for instance, who's stopping at the MacFarlane's place at the head of the glen. From Glasgow University, no less! Our countryside must have some attractions!" She touched her hair absently.

It was Wullie's turn to say "Humph." Funny how Fiona's face always seemed to light up whenever anyone mentioned the name of the young professor from Glasgow. He kept pretty much to himself, smoked a pipe, and took a lot of solitary walks around Glen Duran. Why anyone should come all the way from Glasgow to walk around Glen Duran in the first place was a mystery to Wullie. It simply went to show what happened when a grown man hung around school too long. Not that this Ian Grant was a bad sort, mind you. In fact he was nice. Still, there it was. Why should any-one in his right senses come to a sleepy little High-land village like Abermuir, where nothing ever hap-pened, when he could have all of Glasgow with its noises and excitement to himself? Wullie shook his head and changed the subject.

"Loch Ness will be only twenty miles from here, Fiona. I heard on the radio a man say he saw the monster moving at thirty miles an hour!" His small face brightened. "Do you know what that means, Fiona? It means it could get here in less than an hour! That's if it wanted to."

Her eyebrows went up. "Over land, Wullie? You mean it runs as well as swims?" She shook her head helplessly. "Now please forget the whole thing. How can I read if you keep on talking about monsters that don't exist?"

"But they've got pictures of it," Wullie insisted. "It was in all the papers!"

She said, "Yes, Wullie," without lifting her head, almost as though she hadn't heard him. Perhaps she hadn't.

He turned away in disgust. Big sisters were all the same. Everyone said so. Jamie Gow, who sat next to him in school, had three of them and was some-thing of an expert on the subject. In a way it was strange that the Lord had made so many big sisters

5

and so few monsters. Or maybe he had just got them mixed up. That's what Jamie Gow said and no one knew better than Jamie about big sisters.

Fiona, engrossed in her book, hadn't even bothered to look up when Wullie left. It hardly surprised him. Lately it seemed nobody bothered to look up when he left. Or when he came for that matter.

He dragged his feet through the heather. When summer had started and he had first put aside his shoes, the heather had been coarse and sharp against his tender feet. Now with July almost spent he was no longer aware of the spikey shrub underfoot. As a matter of fact, if truth were told, he was no longer aware of anything. Summer days around Glen Duran were long, with only a few brief hours of darkness to them. Even the small wind that now drifted down from the hills was sluggish and heavy with the scent of bog myrtle and meadowsweet. The birches at the edge of the loch fanned themselves gently in the mid-day heat as he passed. To Wullie they were about the only sign of life as far as the eye could see.

He slumped down morosely by a flat rock which jutted forward from the hill he had been climbing since he left Fiona. A stunted rowan tree served to screen the sun and he eased his back against the cool-ness of the stone. Looking down, he could see far below the whole sweep of Glen Duran. The sered land seemed as though it had been cut out of dun-brown leather and coarse hide. Only Loch Moyne, shimmering in the sun, lent a note of brightness, like a diamond pinned against a somber dress.

Wullie stared again at the loch. It was calm, gold moted in the sunlight, a scene of peace and emptiness. Then suddenly, as he watched, a quick wind blew up and the sky darkened and all the brightness vanished from the water, almost as though, from somewhere under the surface, a great arm had reached up, seized the white glow, and pulled it down into the depths.

But that was impossible, for only some kind of monster deep in Loch Moyne could do that. And there was no monster in Loch Moyne.

Or was there?

CHAPTER TWO

P<small>ROFESSOR</small> Grant's face creased in a slight frown as he passed the plate of oatcakes to the boy. He waved absently in the direction of a slab of cheese and groped in the pocket of his tweed jacket for his pipe. "The Loch Ness Monster, Wullie? What do I think it is?"

"Aye." The boy halted so that the nutty flavor of the oatmeal might caress his tongue. "They wouldn't call it a monster now, if it was something else, would they?"

"Hmmmm." Professor Grant exhaled a wreath of light blue smoke, then tossed the match into the grate. "I've read about it, of course. They say that around a thousand people, at some time or other, claim to have seen it. The trouble is, Wullie, they all seem to differ on what it looks like. It was the newspapers which started to refer to it as the Loch Ness Monster, if I remember correctly." He suddenly smiled. "The skeptics remarked that the creature had a strange way of showing up just around the beginning of the tourist season. Anyway, to answer your question, I'm afraid I wouldn't know what it is—if it's anything."

"Aye, but what do you *think,* Professor?" Wullie prodded. He reached for another oatcake. "If a thousand people saw something, then something must be there."

Ian Grant tapped his pipe against his teeth. "It would appear so," he returned slowly. "You must remember, Wullie, that Loch Ness is no ordinary inland body of water. If some prehistoric marine creature were to exist, the chances for its surviving in a lake such as Loch Ness, are excellent."

"I knew it!" Wullie crowed.

"To start with, Loch Ness is more than seven hundred and fifty feet deep. Deep enough for any large creature. Actually, lakes such as Loch Ness are sea fiords, so they say. Or they were until the land level rose sometime after the ending of the Ice Age. Trapped in such a lake, protected from its natural enemies, a creature from prehistoric times might continue to exist after the last of its species had vanished elsewhere."

"Go on!" Wullie whispered, his eyes round.

"There's really not much more to say. All such a creature would need to survive would be an ample food supply on hand. Anyone who has fished in Loch Ness knows there's no question about that. So there you have it, Wullie. Loch Ness meets all the conditions necessary. It could contain the largest of marine creatures—some sort of sea serpent. And then again there may be nothing there at all. In other words, without facts we can only guess. As a paleontologist I just don't like to guess."

Wullie blinked. "What's that?"

"What's what?"

"What you just said you were?"

"Eh? Oh, a paleontologist?" The young professor smiled. "I'm afraid, Wullie, it's one of these big words that scientists sometimes give themselves to make people think they're a lot more clever than they really are. Actually, in a way you might say that a paleontologist is simply someone who makes a study of old bones."

"Then you'd like fine our dog Tip," Wullie said agreeably. "He's a grand one for old bones too." He was enjoying this chat with his new friend. It was pleasant here in the bright kitchen of the Mac-

Farlane cottage which the professor had rented for the summer. "Fiona doesn't think there's a monster in Loch Ness. You would think, would you not, that she'd have a wee bit more sense? Aye, and her as old as she is besides."

"Fiona? And who, pray, is Fiona?"

"My sister," Wullie said reluctantly, as though confessing to some sort of crime. "She's daft for the books too, like yourself."

"Fiona Watson?" Professor Grant brought his fingers together thoughtfully. "Why now, that wouldn't be the pretty girl with the red hair and green eyes I bumped into coming into the library? And I really mean bumped into! I knocked her books all over the sidewalk. It was when I picked up her library card that I noticed her name."

Wullie stared. "You know her?"

"Unfortunately no. Just met her that once. Good bone structure though." He nodded approvingly to himself then looked at Wullie with renewed interest. "So she's your sister?"

"Aye." Wullie hesitated, not quite sure how to go on. It was strange that Professor Grant had noticed Fiona. Maybe of course the fact that he worked with fossils and old bones explained it. Not that Fiona, old as she was, was really *that* old. Still, plainly she was old enough to have interested the young professor from Glasgow. Wullie frowned. Maybe there was a lot more to this paleontology business than met the eye!

"By the way, Wullie," the professor said with a smile as he saw the boy off, "I don't necessarily agree with your sister, mind you. That is, that there is no monster, or sea serpent, or whatever it is, in Loch Ness. Considering everything we know, there is always a chance that some prehistoric creature is living deep in the lake."

Wullie's face brightened. These were the words he had wanted to hear! And now the professor had spoken them!

"You see, Wullie, millions of years ago all sorts of creatures that have now vanished roamed the earth and sea. We know all this because chalk, which is really a form of colored mud, has told us so. Through the ages millions of plants and animals drifted down to the bottom of the sea. In this mud the bones slowly fossilized. Minerals dripped through them and they took on a permanent hardness. Later, when the water receded, the sea floor was pushed up and became land. That is where our friend the paleontologist comes in. He studies these chalk beds and finds there the remains of plants and animals long since vanished. In a sense you might say he's a detective, though the clues he uses to solve his puzzles are bones millions of years old.

"And that brings us to something else. Sometimes all the clues point in the wrong direction and our scientific detective comes to a wrong conclusion. For instance, take the coelacanth. This peculiar fish, which had paired fins, suggesting the beginning of legs, was supposed to have been extinct for over seventy million years. Scientists would have laughed if anyone had suggested that there was such a thing as a living coelacanth. And then what happened? In 1938 a five-foot coelacanth was brought up from the depths just off the coast of South Africa. It wasn't extinct after all. So it's *possible* that other prehistoric creatures are still living. Deep down in the ocean. Hidden away in a remote lake. I'm not saying, mind you, they *are* there. I just said they *could* be. Good-by, Wullie."

There were many thoughts in Wullie's mind as he made his way home. If what the professor said was true—and who should know better than he?— then some kind of sea monster could be living deep in Loch Ness. And if in Loch Ness, why not in Loch Moyne? The only trouble was, that unlike Loch Ness where a thousand people claimed to have seen something, no one had ever seen anything in Loch Moyne. The thought brought a shadow to the boy's face. It just wasn't fair!

The sun was warm and Wullie's feet dragged as he drew near the pool at the end of the small burn which twisted its way down the hillside. The cool, green turf was inviting to his tired feet, the sparkling water no less to his parched throat. He eased himself down on his stomach and leaned over the shallow bank of the small pool. Cupping his hands, he slurped greedily at the ice chilled water. His thirst assuaged, he rolled over on his back, his head pillowed against a clump of dull green moss. High above, through a tangle of gently waving bracken fronds, he could see the sky, its blueness blunted by the burnished heat cast up from the rock-faced hills. So still and quiet was it where he lay that he could plainly hear the small, individual sounds of the glen: the scolding voice of an inquisitive stonechat from a nearby bush, the soft insistent murmur of the water in the burn as it slipped over and around the smooth round rocks. Slowly Wullie's eyelids began to droop. The sound of his breathing was a far away faintness in his ears now, so that it seemed to come from eons away. His eyes closed and he must have been on the verge of sleep when he was suddenly jolted into wakefulness by a cry for help.

Wullie stared. It was strange. He could have sworn the voice had come from just ahead of him. Only there was no one there. Nor was there anyone to his right. Or to his left. He had almost convinced himself he must have been dreaming when his gaze

14

dropped and he noticed a tiny man struggling to free himself from under a branch which was pinning him to the ground.

Despite his astonishment at seeing such a little man, Wullie got to his feet and quickly freed him from under the fallen branch.

The stranger winced as he rubbed his bruised elbow. He looked up at Wullie and said crossly, "I suppose you expect me to thank you?"

"No," said Wullie. His eyes were popping in his head as he regarded the strange little man. He was dressed in a suit of Lincoln green with mother-of-pearl buttons down the middle. A pair of brown pointed sandals covered his tiny feet. A long green feather extended from the Robin Hood cap which was perched jauntily on his head. His brown face was as wrinkled as a winter apple. His eyes were a fierce blue, with a queer little light to them.

"That hurt," he snapped, as he continued to rub his elbow, almost as though it had been the boy's fault.

"I'm sorry," Wullie said.

"You're sorry?" inquired the little man. "How do you think I feel? I'm the one that tree happened to fall on." He sulked for a moment, his small face a maze of conflicting wrinkles. Finally he squatted down on a flat rock between two small hawthorn bushes and crossed his legs. "Anyway, I'm glad you came along, late as you were!" He paused, then said in a more conversational tone, "What's your name, boy?"

"Wullie. Wullie Watson."

"Wullie Watson?" The little man wrinkled his nose. "Don't like it. Like my own name much better. Of course I'm used to it. Mr. Peebles. I live in the pool over there."

Wullie said nothing. He just gaped. First at the little figure in green. Then at the pool. Suddenly he remembered the stories that Old Fergus MacPhee used to tell the children in the village, stories about the water kelpies who lived in the ancient Highland pools. He, Wullie, had always smiled a little at the stories. He wasn't smiling now. His lips finally moved to let the words squeeze through. "You're a kelpie," he whispered.

"Of course I'm a kelpie," Mr. Peebles replied testily. "What did you think I was? And don't just stand there staring at me!"

"Sorry," mumbled Wullie. He could feel his face go warm under the sour glance of the little man. "I mean it's not every day I meet a kelpie named Mr. Peebles."

The little man seemed to accept the explanation,

16

for the annoyed look left his shriveled face. "I suppose it's not a common name," he said.

Wullie nodded. "Aye, and you being a kelpie besides." He paused, not wishing to offend the quick-tempered little man. "Some people don't believe in kelpies any more," he said carefully.

"I do," Mr. Peebles said crossly.

"Of course," Wullie replied hastily. "You have to!" He paused, then looked curiously at the other. "Is it true, Mr. Peebles, that a kelpie can turn himself into a big black horse? Old Fergus MacPhee said that long ago there was a kelpie in St. Nechtan's pool who was always changing himself into a big black horse."

Mr. Peebles sniffed. "That was my brother-in-law, Calum MacWhurtle! A terrible old show-off. Only what's the use of going around changing yourself into a horse? It doesn't get you anywhere."

Wullie nodded. It made sense.

"Besides, I'd rather be what I am—an honest-to-goodness kelpie. It's suited me fine for two hundred and fifty years."

"Two hundred and fifty years?" gasped Wullie. He goggled at the little man. "You're that old?"

"That's not old," Mr. Peebles said irritably. "I'm only an infant compared with Maggie. Maggie's *old*."

"And who will Maggie be?" inquired Wullie.

"Maggie? The sea monster, of course; the one who lives in Loch Moyne." He looked sharply at Wullie. "Don't you know anything, boy?"

Wullie looked back blankly at the kelpie. His mind was a squirrel cage of leaping, darting thoughts. "But people don't believe in monsters any more," he said finally.

"They don't believe in kelpies either," Mr. Peebles returned snappishly. "I wonder how they'd like it if we didn't believe in them."

Wullie didn't hear him. His thoughts were elsewhere. He could feel the slow, measured *thump—thump—thump* of his heart against his ribs. "A sea monster? In Loch Moyne? Are you sure, Mr. Peebles?"

"Of course, I'm sure! You don't think, Wullie Watson, that I'm likely to get a sea monster mixed up with something else, do you? Her name's Maggie and her family have lived in Loch Moyne for the last hundred million years." He suddenly frowned. "Couldn't tell you where they came from before that."

Wullie said breathlessly, "A hundred million years? She's that old?"

"Not Maggie—her family. I don't know how old Maggie is really. After all, she's a woman and shy about her age. In fact, Maggie's shy about every-

thing. That's why she hardly ever comes to the surface of Loch Moyne. I mean if you were Maggie and knew how everyone feels about monsters, would you want to be stared at?"

Wullie was silent, impressed by Mr. Peebles' logic. "So that's why nobody has ever seen her! And she's been there all the time without anyone knowing it."

Mr. Peebles looked hurt. "I knew it."

CHAPTER THREE

WULLIE sat on the lichened surface of the humpbacked bridge that forded the stream. His feet dangling lazily, he squinted into the sunlight. It was hot and the heat seemed to throb in the motionless air. The glen, freckled with buttercups, lay drowsy in the white glare of the sun. The heat seemed to bend and blur the contour of the scene before him. When one stared long enough, the rocks and the trees seemed to move gently in the air, like wraithlike figures in a dream. There was very little, though, that was dreamlike about the solidly set figure moving resolutely up the trail towards the bridge. Wullie knew who it was before the face came

21

into focus. It was Hector Cruikshank, the owner of Ye Olde Village Tea Shoppe.

Wullie looked away indifferently. He didn't care a great deal for Mr. Cruikshank. Not that the big man with the jutting jaw and the strident voice had ever done anything to him personally. It was just that he didn't like him, although it might have been hard for him to have explained just why. Perhaps it was because Mr. Cruikshank seldom had time for small talk with small boys. In fact all of Mr. Cruikshank's time was spent exclusively on or in the tea room which he had recently opened and which overlooked the loch. He had another small business too, a photograph developing service which he ran in a small room at the back of his restaurant.

Apparently Mr. Cruikshank had been lost in thought and had not noticed the boy sitting quietly on the wall, for he had started when Wullie respectfully hailed him as he approached.

"Eh? Oh, it's you, Wullie Watson!" The big man with the red face mopped his glistening brow with a handkerchief. "Didn't see you for a moment. Thinking. A business man has to think these days. Plenty. Otherwise he doesn't stay in business. No, boy, he doesn't stay in business! Not these days. No sir!"

Mr. Cruikshank always spoke like that. Loudly,

in quick bursts of words. He liked to repeat himself too, as though fascinated by what he had just said. He was a heavily fleshed man, the features of his bulky face set in hard, no-nonsense lines. His long beak of a nose charged well ahead of two small eyes that squinted out from under a protruding ledge of grizzled brow.

"It's hot," Wullie said politely.

"Eh? Hot? Of course it's hot, boy!" Mr. Cruikshank frowned at the dusty trail ahead, fanned himself with his handkerchief, then heaved himself up on the dike beside the boy. He scowled off into space. "Who drinks tea in weather like this?" he asked bitterly. "For that matter, who drinks tea at all in this godforsaken Scottish wilderness? I was out of my mind to have opened a restaurant here. Out of my mind, Wullie Watson! I should have opened it in Edinburgh. That's where all the American tourists go. Loch Ness might have been even better still. My brother-in-law has a tea room there. The man's an idiot! Still there it is. He can't find the time to cart all the money he's making to the bank. Rolling in the stuff. And an idiot!"

Wullie frowned. "And why now will that be, Mr. Cruikshank? Why should the same one be making so much money?"

"Why? Are you stupid, boy, that you don't understand? Have you never heard at all of the Loch Ness Monster?"

"Aye, I have that," Wullie returned.

"Well, that's why! People come from all over to see whatever-it-is in the loch. And while they're there they go to my idiot brother-in-law's place for something to eat and drink." Indignation made his red face even redder and for a moment Wullie was afraid he was going to have some kind of stroke.

"Och, now and that's too bad," Wullie clucked sympathetically. He felt sorry for Mr. Cruikshank. He looked so unhappy!

"Too bad? It's worse than that, boy! Do you know what he sold last week end? I'll tell you. Six hundred and ten cups of tea. Two hundred and sixty-five hot meat pies. Five hundred and twenty-six potato scones. Eighteen dozen oatcakes. It's enough to make a man sick!"

"Aye," agreed Wullie, "it's a lot to eat."

Apparently Mr. Cruikshank hadn't heard him, for he just stared sourly ahead, plainly deep in gloom. Far below, beyond the dun-green strath, Loch Moyne shimmered in the sun. All of the scowls on Hector Cruikshank's big face suddenly bunched together in one massive scowl as he regarded the placid expanse of water in the distance. "It's just not fair at all!" he muttered. "Why couldn't Loch

Moyne have had the monster instead of Loch Ness?''

Wullie opened his mouth, then closed it again. He had just been on the point of telling Mr. Cruikshank about Maggie when something bade him hold his tongue. If he told him about Maggie he would have to tell him about Mr. Peebles, and although the proprietor of Ye Old Village Tea Shoppe might well believe in monsters, Wullie was fairly certain he did not believe in kelpies. No, better keep the news for later.

Hector Cruikshank groaned as he eased his big frame down from the wall. He slapped the dust from his clothes and glowered off in the direction of Loch Moyne. "Six hundred and ten cups of tea! That's where the profit is! And the man's an idiot! I tell you it's just not fair at all." Muttering under his breath, Mr. Cruikshank made his way heavily along the road towards the village, without another glance at the boy.

Wullie sat where he was. His eyes followed the retreating figure until it was lost behind a screen of small larches which struggled for roothold on the hillside. He felt sorry for poor Mr. Cruikshank. He wished there was something he could do that would have helped. But how could he tell Mr. Cruikshank about Maggie without telling him at the same time about Mr. Peebles? Wullie sighed. Life could be difficult at times, as now. Besides, what was the sense of having a monster right in your own back yard if you couldn't enjoy it? Might as well have no monster at all.

He gazed moodily at the loch. Suddenly the surface of the water darkened in one area as the wind came down upon it from out of the mouth of the glen; darkened and gathered itself together into a tight mass. As Wullie watched, his blood cold, the black mass turned at lightning speed and streaked up the loch. Maggie! It had to be! Maggie, lurking just beneath the surface, coyly hiding herself from the eyes of the world, exactly as Mr. Peebles had said!

All at once, as swiftly as it had come, the black shadow on the water was gone. The wind no longer blew from the mouth of the glen.

Loch Moyne shimmered in the sunlight, a scene of peace and emptiness as far as the eye could see.

CHAPTER FOUR

G AVIN WATSON, his spoon halfway to his mouth, frowned as he regarded his son. "What is this Fiona's been telling me, Wullie? Something about your going around saying there's some sort of monster in Loch Moyne?"

Wullie's eyes traveled warily around the breakfast table in the kitchen—first to his mother, then to Fiona, finally back again to his father, sitting directly across the way. "Aye," he said carefully. He salted his porridge and spooned thick yellow cream over the steaming cereal. "Her name's Maggie."

His father's eyebrows went up, while Fiona and her mother exchanged amused glances. "So she has a name?" Mr. Watson inquired drily.

"Aye," Wullie said again. He leaned forward, letting the rising steam from the porridge caress his face. "She's shy, though. That's why nobody ever sees her. She doesn't like to be stared at."

"So that's the reason," Fiona murmured, poker-faced. "And how long has this Maggie been hiding in our loch, Wullie?"

Wullie waited until he had swallowed the spoonful of porridge before answering. "I'll not be knowing for certain. They say, though, that her family have been there for a hundred million years."

Mrs. Watson looked as though she had just choked on a bone, although what a bone would be doing in a bowl of porridge was a mystery. Her face grew red and Wullie wasn't quite sure whether she was laughing or crying.

His father spoke first. And he wasn't laughing. "I think, Wullie, we've had just about enough of this nonsense! Monsters indeed! It all comes from your everlasting daydreaming! Imagination is a fine thing but when a boy goes around mooning over monsters named Maggie it's just too much!"

Wullie shifted his feet under the table and took another spoonful of porridge. It was no use, of course, to mention Mr. Peebles to his father, just as it had been no use mentioning him to Mr. Cruikshank the other day. Besides, his father was the local dominie in the small village school. Schoolmasters didn't believe in anything except maybe homework. Certainly they didn't believe in water kelpies, or at least none that Wullie had ever met. So if he couldn't explain about Mr. Peebles, how could he explain about Maggie? He was sorry now that he had mentioned her to Fiona.

"There, there, Wullie," his mother comforted him, "there's no use at all to fret. Here, help yourself to oatcakes. I'm sure it's all that talk about the Loch Ness Monster that put the idea into your head in the first place. The newspapers have been full of it. Fifty feet long they said it was—whatever it was—"

"Mother!" Fiona's eyebrows arched in surprise and amusement. "Surely you don't believe all that nonsense in the press? It's quite clearly a simple matter of mass hysteria. People see what they want to see. They want to see a monster. So they think they see one. No doubt what they're really looking at is an old mattress, or a log covered with seaweed." She took a sip of her tea. "We studied this type of phenomena in Developmental Psychology."

Wullie glowered. "You and your big books! Still, Professor Grant thinks there could be something in Loch Ness, and he's read a lot more books than you have, Fiona Watson! And if there's something in

29

Loch Ness, then I'm thinking there could be something in Loch Moyne too."

"Professor Grant?" Fiona's cheeks went pink. "You mean the young man from Glasgow? The one who's staying at the MacFarlane cottage?"

Wullie grunted. "How many Professor Grants do you think we have around here, girl? There's only one of them and he's at the MacFarlane place and he said there could be something in the loch!" It felt good to tick off his superior sister. Aye, and with all her fancy courses!

"Professor Grant?" murmured Fiona. There was a faraway look in her green eyes and she seemed to have forgotten all about her breakfast. She darted a suspicious look at her small brother. "I hope you weren't talking about me, Wullie?"

"As a matter of fact," Wullie returned airily, "we were talking about old bones and your name happened to come up."

Fiona stared at him aghast. Her voice was almost a wail. "Oh no!" She looked for a moment as though she was about to cry.

Wullie nibbled thoughtfully at the corner of his oatcake. He always ate the corners first. "I'm not understanding, though, how he can keep that grand job he has in Glasgow and him with such bad eyes."

He frowned. "Got you mixed up with some nice looking girl with red hair he bumped into coming out of the library."

Fiona's face was no longer pink. It was a deep red. "That was me!" she cried. Her eyes danced with excitement. "Did he really say that, Wullie? I mean about my being nice looking? I know you were only teasing about the old bones."

Mr. Watson sighed as he slid back his chair from the table. "I need a rest. First it was monsters. Then it's old bones. And today I met Hector Cruikshank and all he kept mumbling about was six hundred and ten cups of tea!" He crossed over and tossed a handful of bog fir on the smoldering peats in the fire. He watched, a frown on his normally good-natured face, as the flames licked up the sides of the big black kettle that hung from the pothook. "Anyway, Wullie, I want no more talk about any weird creature in Loch Moyne. Do you understand?"

"But—"

"I said, Wullie, do you understand?" Mr. Watson's voice was grim.

Wullie lowered his eyes before his father's steely gaze. He sank his teeth into the remaining corner of his oatcake. "Aye," he said.

Strangely enough he did not say it dispiritedly.

As a matter of fact he rather agreed with his father. There was no sense at all in just talking any more about the monster who lived in Loch Moyne.

It was time to do something about it.

Mr. Peebles squatted on the small flat stone between the two hawthorn bushes and regarded the boy huffily.

"You mean you don't believe there's a monster in the loch, is that it, boy?"

Wullie pretended a show of embarrassment. He shifted his weight uncomfortably, careful not to step on the kelpie. Mr. Peebles looked bad-tempered enough. "Well, it's yourself, Mr. Peebles, who will be knowing that nobody has really seen the monster."

"I've seen her!" Mr. Peebles snapped. He tossed a twig into the pool and watched the small circles widen.

"Of course!" Wullie agreed hastily. "It's just that, well, you're not people—"

"Thank goodness for that! It's bad enough at times just being a kelpie!" He got to his feet and stood lost in thought for a long moment. Suddenly he seemed to come to a decision. A sly smile wreathed his mouth. "I suppose you won't believe there's a monster in Loch Moyne until you see her for yourself. Very well, Wullie Watson. Just off shore from the ruins of Lamont Castle—be there tomorrow morning at ten. There shouldn't be anyone around at that hour. I'll tell Maggie to show up."

"Oh," said Wullie. He had hardly expected such a prompt reaction.

Mr. Peebles' eyes gleamed mischievously. "What's the matter? You look a little pale, boy. Anything wrong? I mean you're not afraid of a monster, are you, Wullie Watson?

The boy ran his tongue across his parched lips. Now that the plan had worked he was suddenly aware of an enormous fear deep inside him. What on earth had possessed him to make such a daft appointment? With a monster, no less, and in the quietest, most solitary loch in all Scotland? Aye, and at an hour when no one would be around. Just the two of them: he, Wullie Watson, and the Loch Moyne Monster. That is, if you didn't count Mr. Peebles. And Wullie knew in his heart he could scarcely expect much help from a two hundred and fifty-year-old kelpie.

So lost in black thoughts had Wullie been that he did not notice when Mr. Peebles disappeared into the pool where he lived. It was only after the kelpie had vanished that Wullie looked around and realized he had gone.

"Mr. Peebles!" he cried, a tremor of uneasiness

in his voice. "Och, now and it was only a wee joke I was having! Tell Maggie there's no need at all to bother herself. Fine I know she's busy—"

He stopped. The kelpie was gone—gone as though he had stepped into another world, as perhaps he had. Too late to call him back. Perhaps even now, through some subterranean passage leading from the pool to the loch, he was already in touch with the monster, telling her, at this very moment of the meeting in the morning. Wullie groaned. What an idiot he had been! Of course he could always stay home and simply forget the whole business. After all no one would know the difference. No one that is, except Mr. Peebles.

Except Mr. Peebles. Yes, *he* would know. He would know the reason if Wullie failed to be there in the morning. He would know that for all his big talk, he, Wullie Watson, was a braggart with the heart of an April lamb. And even though the other was just a kelpie, and a not very gracious one besides, Wullie knew in his heart he could not bear to have the little man think him a coward.

The boy sighed. It all came from talking too much. After all, who really cared around Abermuir whether or not there was a monster in Loch Moyne? Maybe Mr. Cruikshank did, but only because it might help him sell more tea and scones. But after

Mr. Cruikshank, who else cared? Nobody. Nobody that is except—

Wullie paused. There was someone else who cared! Someone who would care a great deal should there be a monster in Loch Moyne. That someone was Professor Ian Grant, the young scientist from Glasgow.

CHAPTER FIVE

I AN GRANT scowled slightly as he followed the boy along the briar-choked trail that squirmed down to the ruins of Lamont Castle on the edge of the loch. The path was narrow and it was difficult to avoid the nettles underfoot and the massed bramble bushes that crowded in from each side. It was so difficult that after a while the young scientist stopped trying, plainly resigned to the thorns that scraped his face and hands and the thistles and nettles that tore at his trousers.

"I must be crazy," he muttered to himself as he struggled to free the strap of his camera from a sinuous vine. "Me, Ian Grant, Assistant Professor of Paleontology at the University of Glasgow, out on a monster hunt! And why? Because some kid talks me into it. And how does the kid know there's a monster in Loch Moyne? Simple! A two hundred and fifty-year-old kelpie by the name of Mr. Peebles told him, that's why!" The young professor sighed. "I just hope nobody finds out about this at the university."

Wullie slowed and looked back over his shoulder at the grim figure threshing through the underbrush. "Are you all right, Professor?"

Ian Grant nodded. "Except for a dozen minor lacerations, I never felt better, Wullie. It's my head I'm really worried about."

The boy looked concerned. "Och now, and is there anything wrong with it?"

The man forced a grin. "I don't know for certain. It seemed all right before I set out on this crazy safari. But that's not your fault. I shouldn't really have let you talk me into it." A quick smile suddenly relaxed the serious cast of his young face. "Still, anyone who has a good-looking sister with red hair and green eyes can be awfully persuasive at times. Lead on, Wullie!"

The boy frowned, not quite sure what Fiona had to do with all this. He was glad, though, that the professor had finally agreed to come along with him. Not that he had seemed terribly enthusiastic at first. Especially when he found out about the two hundred and fifty-year-old kelpie who lived in the pool overlooking the loch. That had jarred him a little. It was rather clear to Wullie that the professor had done a lot more reading about prehistoric monsters than he had about present-day kelpies. In the end, though, after gulping down a cup of hot coffee he had shaken his head, sighed, and reached for the camera he always took with him on his travels around the countryside. "Okay, Wullie," he had said finally, "let's go. This camera has a special wide angle lens so we'll be sure to get all of your monster in the picture." Overjoyed that he would not be alone when Maggie appeared, Wullie had rushed out of the cottage before the professor got a chance to change his mind.

They paused to catch their breath when they reached a spot directly above Lamont Castle. All of the original walls of the grim fortress that once commanded the approaches to Loch Moyne had long since sagged into ruin. Slender ribbons of ivy slithered across the fire-scourged stones like green-scaled serpents. To the right of the castle, a briary strip of land, narrow at the end, jutted out into the loch like a pointed knife. Apparently the small peninsula had at one time been used as a graveyard, for a considerable number of tombstones, ravaged by time, lay tilted and toppled in all directions. The scene below was one of incredible destruction, as though some mad giant long ago had stormed down from the mountains and pulled Lamont Castle apart with demoniac hands. Nothing apparently had escaped, and certainly not the pathetic little grave-yard. The white headstones, smoothed by wind and rain, lay scattered on the ground like clean-picked bones. It was a scene of desolation and death; a scene to chill the blood even on the warmest of days. Wullie was more than ever glad that Professor Grant had agreed to come along.

Ian Grant glanced at his watch. "Half-past nine. We've got thirty minutes yet." He glowered at the huge heap of crumbling stone beneath them. "Can't say I particularly approve of your meeting place, Wullie. Couldn't your Mr. Peebles have arranged for this monster of yours to have shown herself in a somewhat more accessible spot? Just look at that rubble heap ahead of us! It's enough to give a mountain goat vertigo! And after we cross that, we have to fight our way through a jungle of weeds and tombstones to the end of that little point of land." He grunted. "If that monster does show up I'm going to be so exhausted I won't have enough strength left to click the camera."

Wullie thought it best to explain. "Maggie's shy. She doesn't like at all to have people staring at her. That's what Mr. Peebles said."

"Ah, yes, Mr. Peebles." Ian Grant closed his eyes

for a moment. He sighed for the tenth time that morning. "I had forgotten about him." He seemed to come to a quick decision for he turned and eyed the boy sternly. "Wullie, it's about time I told you frankly that I think this whole affair is sheer idiocy. There's no monster in Loch Moyne, and you know it! Yes, and all this talk about little men in green suits who can change themselves into black horses! I don't care if your Mr. Peebles is five hundred and fifty years old, he never saw a monster named Maggie in Loch Moyne!"

"But—

"Okay, Wullie, forget it. I don't really blame you. I agreed to go on this monster hunt and we might as well finish it."

He looked so unhappy that Wullie thought it best not to argue. Silently he followed the lean figure of the young professor down the trail. Soon they were scrambling and sliding over the massive stones of Lamont Castle. Quite plainly Ian Grant did little climbing around Glasgow University, for on at least six occasions he lost his footing around the scree and loose rock and went crashing to the ground. Each time he fell he made various comments under his breath in a language Wullie did not understand and which he figured must be Latin, Professor Grant being such a grand scholar and all! He seemed out

of sorts, though, and his disposition was not notice-
ably improved when they reached the graveyard
only to find a hungry swarm of small stinging midges
waiting for them on the tussocky grass. Wullie was
relieved when they finally fought their way to the
tip of the narrow peninsula.

Ian Grant sank wearily to the ground and leaned
his back against a tilted tombstone. His face glistened with sweat and a number of angry welts had
started to appear on his forehead. His trousers and
shirt were torn in a dozen places where he had fallen.
A host of angry looking insect bites covered his arms
and neck. He looked woebegone.

Wullie cast an anxious glance at the slumped
figure by the tombstone. He hoped Professor Grant
was not really angry about anything. He had been
somewhat shocked, though, to hear his new friend
say what he had about there being no monster in
Loch Moyne. Aye, and him a professor too, and a
great one for the books besides! Still maybe the man
wasn't quite himself this morning. Wullie had
noticed he had looked a little strange once or twice
during the descent to the loch. Maybe he should
have chosen the longer, but much simpler route that
brought one past Mr. Cruikshank's tea room. Wullie
made a mental note to do just that on their next visit.

Ian Grant stirred. Painfully he raised his right

arm and regarded his watch from under swollen eyelids. "Three minutes after ten." He glanced around. Loch Moyne was as still and devoid of life as the graveyard of Lamont Castle. "She's late," he said laconically. "Like all women." He cast another careless glance around the deserted loch, then jammed his rolled up jacket under his head. He leaned back against the tombstone. "Don't forget to wake me if she shows up, Wullie. Wouldn't miss it for anything. You can't miss her. A monster. Answers to the name of Maggie." His head went back and his eyes closed.

"But—" Wullie cried before he noticed that the young professor was already asleep. The boy stared around uneasily. He did not exactly relish being alone at a moment like this. Not that he was alone really. The professor was still there, if asleep, only a few feet away. Still—Wullie's eyes, just a little frightened, flickered over the surface of Loch Moyne. Nothing stirred in the long sweep of unbroken and luminous water that surrounded them. Nothing. A low mass of clouds suddenly swept above the scene, driving a long wedge of gray into the brightness of the loch. Two white gulls, like drifting flecks of down in the half light, glided over the ruins of Lamont Castle. Their plaintive cries still trembled in the still air after the birds had vanished.

Slowly, as the moments passed and nothing happened, Wullie felt the first stirrings of doubt deep within him. The angry clouds had rushed away and Loch Moyne sparkled again in the sunlight. Mr. Peebles had said ten o'clock, and it was now ten-fifteen. Almost surely the professor had been right after all. Aye, and Fiona too, Wullie reflected grimly. There was no monster in Loch Moyne. There never had been. The boy, his eyes red and strained from staring at the empty water, was just on the point of waking the professor and starting for home when suddenly, about fifty feet from shore, he noticed it. A slight ripple in the endless sheen of smooth water. *Almost as though, just under the surface of the loch, something was gliding soundlessly towards where he was sitting!*

He was on his feet, staring. His breath was a hot lump in his throat and he tried to cry out but couldn't. He stood waiting, his legs trembling, sweat on the palms of his hands. Then just when the dark shadow sweeping towards him was about twenty feet away, the polished surface of the water was broken and a small flat head appeared. It was a head the like of which Wullie, in all his life, had never seen. The nostrils were set high up on the skull, between two unblinking eyes. Just behind them was another opening where a third equally unblinking eye was lodged. The mouth was slightly opened, revealing a set of small but strong, conical teeth. Then as

Wullie watched, and Professor Grant slept, a slender snakelike neck, oscillating gently, emerged from the water. It was followed a moment later by a squat body, not unlike that of a turtle. On each side of the smooth, scaleless body were two strange looking flippers by which the creature glided forward and backward in the water. A stubby tail, less than a foot long, seemed to act as a rudder as the thing, whatever it was, skimmed over the surface of the loch.

Wullie's startled eyes traveled slowly from the small flat head perched at the end of the swaying neck to the stubby tail. Then they traveled back, just in case they had missed something the first time. Only they hadn't. That was all there was to the monster. But who ever heard of a monster just five feet long, and more than half of that, neck?

"Professor!" he cried, his voice returning with his courage, "there's something in the water out there! Some queer kind of turtle with a long neck and three eyes."

"Eh? Turtle?" mumbled the professor. He yawned, grumbled under his breath and was just about to make himself more comfortable when his entire body seemed to freeze. One eye was shut. One eye was open. And the one that was open was staring in disbelief at Loch Moyne.

"It can't be!" muttered Ian Grant. "It's not possible!" The next second he was scrambling to his feet, clawing feverishly for his camera. Like a man possessed, he threshed around in the bracken where he had placed it before he went to sleep. A triumphant shout burst from his lips as his groping fingers found it. With a bound he was past Wullie, his fingers making quick adjustments to the camera as he got to the water's edge. He had only taken one picture when the creature, apparently startled by the clamor, turned and raced away. It must have been traveling at a speed of about ten miles an hour when suddenly it slipped down beneath the surface. Only a tiny wake marked the spot where it had been.

Professor Grant's face was white, almost as though he had just seen a ghost. He stared unbelievingly at the spot where the small creature had vanished into the depths of Loch Moyne. Finally the expression of shock seemed to leave his eyes. It was replaced by one of unconcealed bitterness. He shook his dark head savagely. "Idiot! Imbecile! Nincompoop!"

Wullie blanched. He had never dreamed that his new friend, normally so mild-mannered, would take it so badly. After all, it was hardly his fault that the monster had turned out to be anything but a monster. Of course he should really have asked Mr. Peebles how big Maggie was. He had simply supposed that being a monster she would be at least fifty feet long.

"It's sorry I am," Wullie whispered unhappily. He didn't have the courage to face the professor. In all his life he had never felt quite so miserable. Not for himself, although it was bad enough that the monster had been such a disappointment after all his high hopes. It was for Professor Grant that he really felt sorry. Dragging him out of bed on his holiday on a wild monster chase! And all the poor man had to show for it was a mass of bruises, stings, and a frayed disposition.

"Eh?" Ian Grant inquired absently. He looked puzzled for a moment as though his thoughts had been elsewhere. Suddenly a small fan of wrinkles bunched around his gray eyes as he smiled. "Come now, Wullie, it's not you who's the imbecile, it's me! Sleeping like a fat lazy cat in the sun! I should have been awake!"

Wullie frowned. He looked uncertainly from the professor back to the spot in the loch where the small creature had vanished. It was hard to understand what Professor Grant should be so disturbed about. He had scarcely missed anything. A queer little creature, half neck, half flippers. Nothing to get excited about. It was certainly not the great monster that Wullie had promised and that he had expected to

see after his talk with Mr. Peebles. He glowered now
as he remembered how the little man had tricked
him yesterday. "You're not afraid of a monster, are
you, Wullie Watson?" Mr. Peebles had inquired
craftily. Och, and they were sly ones altogether, were
the kelpies!

Professor Grant was still looking blankly at the
loch. He seemed lost in thought. "I don't suppose,
Wullie," he said slowly, after a long silence, "that
you ever heard of a plesiosaur, have you?"

"Eh?" Wullie inquired. "A who?"

"A plesiosaur. But of course you haven't! It was
a prehistoric marine reptile that once roamed the
earth. You see, eons ago a great many creatures
which had always lived on land, gradually made the
transition to the sea. Some became equally at home
on both land and in the sea, like our friends, the
turtle and the crocodile. The plesiosaur too made
the transition. It had nostrils high on its head and
could breathe on the surface while remaining hidden under the water." He paused, then added slowly,
"According to scientists, Wullie, the last plesiosaur
became extinct a hundred million years ago."

The boy frowned. "So?"

Ian Grant scratched his head uncertainly. "So I
guess I'm going crazy, Wullie," he said, "but I could
have sworn I just saw one five minutes ago!"

47

CHAPTER SIX

IT was the following day, just before tea time, that the knocker struck on the door of the Watson cottage. Wullie got to the door first. Wullie always got to the door first. He threw it open. "Professor Grant!" he exclaimed with pleasure as he recognized the caller.

"Sorry to bother you folks," the young professor said as he shook hands with Mr. and Mrs. Watson. "I've wanted to meet you for some time. Wullie here is a good friend of mine."

"That's right," Wullie agreed.

Ian Grant's eyes strayed innocently to where Fiona was sitting, somewhat tense, by the fire. "As for your daughter, we met once before. Outside the Abermuir Free Library, as I remember it."

A quick tide of color rose in the girl's face. Before she could say anything, though, Mrs. Watson had the caller firmly in tow and seated at the table with a tea cup in front of him.

"So you're staying at the MacFarlane place? Well, now! They're fine people, the MacFarlanes. Sugar? A wee bit of milk, of course? Fiona was after telling me she had met a nice young man from Glasgow by the library—"

"Mother!" exclaimed Fiona, her face a beet red.

"Hush yourself!" Nan Watson admonished with a wave of her plump arm. "It's plain to see that Mr. Grant is a nice young man." She poured the tea. "I'm only sorry to hear, though, that our Wullie has been making something of a nuisance of himself since you got here. The boy's plain daft about sea monsters. Of course you'll be minding yourself that it's been in all the papers about the strange creature they've supposed to have over in Loch Ness. I'm afraid Wullie's not been himself at all since the stories got around."

"That's right, Nan," Mr. Watson agreed. He lit his pipe and tossed the match into the fireplace. "This is rather a small community we have here. An older one too, I'm afraid. Not many boys around who are Wullie's age and not a great deal to do now that school is out. So after he's done his chores around the cottage he's got nothing much to do but to daydream. Mostly about sea monsters, I understand. Just sorry he's been bothering you."

Ian Grant took a sip of his tea and shook his head. "He's not been bothering me, Mr. Watson. As a matter of fact, he's been quite a help to me. You see, I'm a paleontologist. I dig old bones." He smiled. "That's one of the small jokes I use in my introductory speech to the new classes, just to show I'm hep to what's happening. Anyway, Wullie got me quite interested when he said there was something in Loch Moyne."

Mrs. Watson shook her head vigorously as she passed a plate of potato scones and butter to the guest. "Loch Moyne! Never the day! I've lived here all my life and I should know. The only thing in Loch Moyne is water."

"It's an interesting loch just the same, Mrs. Watson," Ian Grant said. "After all any inland body of water more than seven hundred and fifty feet deep is interesting. Besides that, Loch Moyne lies squarely in the middle of the geologic fault that splits Scotland from east to west. In addition, it once had an opening to the oceans of the world. That raises all sorts of intriguing possibilities. That's why I say, speaking from a strictly zoological point of view, if some heretofore undiscovered form of prehistoric marine life were to be found today, the conditions for its being found in Loch Moyne are as good as any."

Fiona's brows came together in a small frown. "But aren't the same conditions present in Loch Ness?

"That's right, Fiona," Ian Grant agreed.

"But surely you don't believe all those old wives' tales about the Loch Ness Monster?" the girl cried in horror. She wrinkled her pert nose. "It's—it's unscientific!"

"I suppose you're right." Ian Grant shrugged slightly. "Still, there it is, Fiona. In a sense, scientists are only men asking questions. And frankly there's an awful lot of answers they haven't come up with yet." He paused and rolled his buttered potato scone. "Just the same every week, somewhere, we learn something new. For instance, it's difficult for us to realize that it wasn't until as late as 1847 that the world learned there was such an animal as the gorilla. We only discovered the giant panda in 1869 and the okapi in 1901. In other words, these creatures had been going about their business for thousands of centuries, yet as far as the world of science was concerned they didn't exist. So you can be rather certain that right at this moment, somewhere other forms of marine and animal life exist that we haven't even dreamed about."

"But Loch Moyne?" Fiona asked doubtfully. She hesitated. "Wullie was saying he saw something yesterday. Some queer kind of turtle with a long neck. Of course Wullie's always seeing something." She hurried on somewhat apologetically. "He's got quite an imagination, has Wullie."

"I haven't," Professor Grant said quietly, "and I saw it too."

"Saw what?" Mr. Watson inquired.

Ian Grant hesitated as though searching for the right words. "I wasn't quite sure," he said slowly. "It was simply impossible for me to believe what my senses were telling me. After all, if what I was thinking was correct, then I was face to face with a form of life that scientists were certain had vanished from the earth a hundred million years ago."

No one spoke in the kitchen. The only sound was the rhythmic tick-tock of the wag-o'-the-wall clock over the chest of drawers and the small shushing sound as a burned peat sank deeper into the ashes in the fireplace.

"It was too incredible to believe. Then I remembered the one shot I had been able to take before the thing sank under the water. I couldn't be certain, of course, that the picture would come out, or for that matter whether in my excitement I had missed the creature altogether and had taken an interesting shot of Loch Moye at ten o'clock in the morning. I can tell you I was running a real fever until I picked up the print today from the studio that Mr. Cruikshank runs behind his tea room." He paused. "It was everything I had hoped and prayed for. There in the center of the picture was the unmistakable image of what I can only believe was a plesiosaur."

"That's right," Wullie added. In a way he was a little surprised that Professor Grant should be making such a fuss over the whole business. The small creature had been a sad disappointment as a monster. If Maggie was a typical example of what a plesiosaur must have looked like, it was no wonder that everyone had figured they had vanished a hundred million years ago.

"A plesiosaur?" Mr. Watson inquired thoughtfully. "It seems to me I've heard of it. Wasn't it some kind of reptile?"

"That's right, Mr. Watson. Actually the plesiosaur didn't swim like a fish; it paddled through the water like a duck. On each side of its body it had two powerful flippers about six feet long. With these flippers, or paddles, it could go backwards or forwards, something like an ancient Roman galley. A distinctive feature of the plesiosaur was its long, snakelike neck. As a matter of fact the proportion of neck to body is greater than in any known animal, including the giraffe. The plesiosaur was no pigmy either—many of them were fifty feet and longer."

Wullie looked up, suddenly interested. "You mean maybe Maggie's still growing?" he asked hopefully.

"Maybe." Professor Grant grinned. "I can't guarantee, though, that she'll be any bigger than she is now, Wullie. Incidentally, I can't guarantee either at this moment that she is a plesiosaur, although I firmly believe she is. Anyway, I need some additional information. I've already sent a telegram to a colleague at the London Museum and I imagine in a few days I'll have to go down there personally." He chuckled. "I can just see old Dr. Smithers when he gets my wire. He'll probably think I've been drinking too much *usquebaugh* up here in the Highlands."

"Amazing!" Mr. Watson exclaimed. "Simply amazing! A plesiosaur. And right in our own Loch Moyne!"

"Her name's Maggie," Wullie said matter-of-factly. "She's shy. That's why nobody has ever seen her."

Ian Grant got to his feet. "Sorry to have bothered

you folks," he said apologetically. "I keep forgetting I'm not in the classroom. I also keep forgetting that, outside of the scientific community, no one is really too much interested in such matters. And after all, why should they be? So if I've been carried away a little bit, I hope you'll forgive me."

"But we *are* interested!" Fiona cried breathlessly, her eyes wide with excitement as she gazed at the young professor. There was a spot of color on her cheeks as she leaned forward in her chair, her hands clasped in front of her. "Is there anything we can do to help?"

"Help?" He turned, then shook his head. "Not really, Fiona, but thanks just the same. Maybe, though, it would be best that no one said too much about this until I get in touch with Dr. Smithers. He's one of the foremost authorities on the Mesozoic period. I'd like another opinion before making any public statement." He opened the door. "Thanks for the tea, Mrs. Watson. Good-by." With a quick wave he drew the door shut behind him.

There was a long silence after he had left. It was Fiona who spoke first. There was a faraway look in her eyes. "What a discovery!" She sighed. "I think he's handsome."

"It's a she," Wullie pointed out firmly. "Her name's Maggie."

"Please shut up, Wullie," Fiona murmured dreamily. "I'm not talking about your discovery. I'm talking about mine. About Professor Grant."

"Nice young man," Mr. Watson said, rapping his pipe in the palm of his hand. "I like the way he speaks and carries himself. We could use more like him around here."

"Lots more," Fiona agreed, the same faraway look in her eyes.

Mrs. Watson cast a disapproving glance at her daughter. "Don't be so forward, Fiona Watson! Sometimes I can't understand you young people nowadays. Believe me, it was a lot different when I was a girl."

Fiona sighed blissfully. Her eyes closed. "But the world doesn't really change, Mother. Even in a hundred million years. Just think! For ages and ages people went to bed every night thinking that the last plesiosaur had flipped its last flipper. And all the time the cunning rascals were hiding out right here in our Loch Moyne. Or at least one of them was."

Mrs. Watson picked up the lambskin which she had already scraped and cured and would later fashion into a pair of slippers for Wullie. She seated herself by the fire and reached for the glasses she always wore when she worked. "Anyway, Fiona, I'm thinking the whole business is hardly that important. As that nice young man just said, it's really only of interest to the scientific community." She ran her fingers across the lambskin. "Whatever that is."

Wullie sat quite still. Thinking. Had what his mother just said been really true? Were only scientists interested in the fact that there might be a plesiosaur in Loch Moyne? A trickle of resentment made its way along his nerves. Any creature who had managed to hang around for a hundred million years deserved some kind of recognition. Yet nobody really seemed to care. Of course, Professor Grant did, but he was different. Besides he was an outsider, from Glasgow. He would hardly be expected to show a local pride in the fact that the last plesiosaur on earth had chosen Loch Moyne as its home.

Wullie scowled into the flames. It just wasn't fair! In all of Abermuir, no one who cared whether or not there was a plesiosaur in Loch Moyne! No one— He paused as memory suddenly pressed a button in his brain. No one? But of course there was! Someone who only a few days ago had been bewailing the fact that Loch Moyne had no monster like the one reputed to be in Loch Ness.

Hector Cruikshank, the proprietor of Ye Olde Village Tea Shoppe, cared.

CHAPTER SEVEN

ECTOR CRUIKSHANK sat at the empty table in the empty dining room of his small restaurant and moodily regarded the boy in front of him.

"So it's you, Wullie Watson?" He frowned. "I doubt you've come here to buy a cup of tea. If you have I must tell you that we have no special servings for children. It's the same price for everyone, man and boy. Eightpence the cup."

"I didn't come here for tea," Wullie explained. "I've got something to tell you."

"Then tell it," Mr. Cruikshank said irritably. He pushed back his chair, served himself a cup of tea and rang up eightpence on the cash register. "On top of everything else, my books don't balance," he muttered under his breath as he waved Wullie to a table. He seated himself across from the boy and stirred his beverage. "You said you had something to tell me?"

Wullie nodded. "It's about the monster."

"The what?"

"The monster. The one in Loch Moyne," Wullie said conversationally. "Professor Grant says it's something called a plesiosaur. The last time anyone ever saw one was around a hundred million years ago."

The proprietor of Ye Olde Village Tea Shoppe looked as though he was about to have some kind of fit. His cheeks grew flushed and he seemed to be having trouble swallowing his tea. Perhaps it was too hot, Wullie thought. He felt sorry for the poor man. Something always seemed to be happening to Mr. Cruikshank!

"A monster?" the man finally exclaimed. "Did you say a monster, boy?"

"I did that," Wullie said.

"In Loch Moyne?"

"Aye. In Loch Moyne." He looked around hopefully and his eyes lingered on the iced cakes on the counter. Mr. Cruikshank did not take the hint. Quite apparently his thoughts were elsewhere.

"From the beginning, Wullie Watson," he said slowly. "The whole story." He poured himself an-

other cup of tea and after a moment's hesitation rang up another eightpence. He caught the boy's questioning glance. "You'll observe, boy, that I play no favorites. I pay for my own tea. You'll understand then that I could hardly give it to you for nothing."

"Of course," Wullie agreed hastily. "I mean, that wouldn't be fair at all!"

"Nevertheless, you're welcome to a glass of fresh water over there." The big man made his way back to the table. He stirred the cup and eyed the boy suspiciously. "Now what's all this about Professor Grant? He was here yesterday for some picture I developed for him."

"That was it," Wullie said. "That was the monster."

Mr. Cruikshank sat quite still. His eyes narrowed. His spoon continued to make rhythmic patterns in his cup. "Go on, Wullie Watson," he said softly. "I'm listening."

And listen he did, raptly, and without interruption until the boy had finished. Then he had Wullie repeat the story, as though to test the accuracy of the facts as he had been given them the first time. Only then did Hector Cruikshank get to his feet. There was a crafty gleam in his small eyes as he made his way to the adjoining studio. He emerged with

61

a triumphant shout a moment later, a white square of paper in his hand.

"I wasn't quite satisfied with the first print I made for Professor Grant, so I made another one, the one he has now. Of course I didn't pay too much attention to what the picture was all about." He stared for a long moment at the photograph in his hand, a curious little smile around his fleshy lips, before passing it to the boy. "Be careful. That's a valuable picture you have there, Wullie Watson. A very valuable picture!"

Wullie nodded, not quite understanding. It was hard to see what could be so valuable about it. After all, Professor Grant had the negative. And the picture itself, as far as Wullie could see, was nothing to get excited about. True, you could clearly see the four flippers and the funny little head perched at the end of the queer neck. It was just that Maggie looked no bigger in the photograph than she had looked in Loch Moyne. In fact she looked even smaller.

Mr. Cruikshank took the picture back from the boy. He seemed pleased about something and he hummed as he regarded the creature in the picture. "Well, well, so that's a plesiosaur?"

"She's a small one," Wullie confessed. "Professor Grant said that they grew to a length of fifty feet, aye, and more than that even. Of course that was a hundred million years ago."

"Well, we can hardly wait *that* long, can we, Wullie?" Mr. Cruikshank said cheerfully, his face creased in a big smile. "Maybe we can do something to make her grow a little faster, eh?" He rubbed his hands together.

Wullie stared at him. Had the man taken leave of his senses? There was a big difference between five feet and fifty feet; forty-five feet to be exact. How long it had taken Maggie to reach her present size, there was no way of knowing. Plesiosaurs didn't grow at the same rate as people. For that matter neither did kelpies, Wullie reflected, remembering Mr. Peebles. The boy frowned.

"How will you do that, Mr. Cruikshank?" he asked curiously.

"Eh? Do what?"

"Make Maggie grow faster? Mr. Peebles said that Maggie is older than he is, and the same one is two hundred and fifty years old. If she's only five feet now I'm thinking it's going to be a long while before she's a full grown monster."

"That's right." Mr. Cruikshank laughed deep in his throat and closed his left eye in a knowing wink. "Let's see now. Five into two hundred and fifty, that's fifty. What you're saying, Wullie, is that according to your friend Mr. Peebles Maggie has grown at the rate of one foot every fifty years. If she keeps that up, it would take her twenty-five hundred years altogether before she's a full-sized fifty-foot monster." He shook his head. "We just can't wait that long. We need our monster now, Wullie, if she's going to do us any good." His eyes traveled around the empty tea room. "And believe me, she's going to do us a lot of good!"

Wullie looked puzzled. "I'm not understanding at all, Mr. Cruikshank."

The man waved an impatient hand, all the former good humor gone from his face. "I'm not asking you to understand! I'm handling matters. And as for that Mr. Peebles you keep talking about, the less said about him, from now on, the better. It's all right believing in monsters. After all, we've got all the scientists to back us up. But nobody believes in kelpies. Not even scientists. You listen to me, Wullie Watson. If we start going around yapping about funny little men in green coats, the newspapers will think the whole thing's some kind of joke. I intend to keep everything on a high level! A strictly scientific level." He paused, then said dramatically, "And we've got everything we need to make it just that! A genuine monster. A genuine photo of the monster. And a genuine scientist who saw the monster!"

"But, Mr. Cruikshank—" Wullie began as the man took him by the arm and gently but firmly steered him towards the door—"I'm not finished yet!"

"I am! And don't you worry about the size of the little lady in the loch. When I get done retouching and blowing up that print I have, Maggie will be so big she'll make the *Queen Elizabeth II* look like a tugboat alongside her." He thrust a stale raisin cake into the boy's hand. "Here's something for you, Wullie. Now on your way! I've got lots to do!"

The boy made his way home slowly, his feet dragging. He was not quite sure he understood everything Mr. Cruikshank had said. All that business about making Maggie look like a full grown monster! What he did understand left him with a vague feeling of uneasiness. He had realized, of course, that in speaking to him in the first place about Maggie he had ignored Professor Grant's request to say nothing until he could check with the London experts. True, he had only meant to enlist the help of Mr. Cruikshank in seeing that Maggie got some recognition around Abermuir. But only around Abermuir. What he had not meant to do was to get Mr. Cruikshank so excited as to do something that might harm the professor. The last thing Wullie would have wanted was to hurt his new friend in any way. Still, as he trudged back to Abermuir he could not shake the vague feeling of uneasiness, and the thought that by telling Hector Cruikshank about Maggie and the professor, he had set in motion forces he was now powerless to stop.

CHAPTER EIGHT

H M—" Professor Grant tugged gently at the lobe of his right ear. It was a habit he had whenever something was on his mind. Something plainly was on his mind now as he stared out of the cottage window. Finally, a tiny smile loosened his mouth as he turned to the boy. Wullie sat hunched forward on a chair, his face tight with misery.

"Forget it, Wullie," the man said with a shrug. "I know you didn't mean any harm. In any event I don't own Maggie. I imagine I do own that print which Mr. Cruikshank has, although I'm afraid I would need a lawyer to prove the point." He stuffed a few shreds of tobacco into his pipe and scraped a match. "Frankly, I'd just as soon not get involved in any courtroom action at this time. For one reason, I'm on my holidays. For another, I don't think the university would like it." He exhaled a feather of light-blue smoke. "So let's see what happens."

"Aye, but it's happened," Wullie said, his voice breaking in his throat. "Fiona just told me. Mr. Cruikshank made a blow-up of the picture. He sent it this morning to the newspapers in Glasgow and Edinburgh." He choked. "The picture makes Maggie look like—like a monster. You wouldn't know her at all."

Ian Grant said drily, "That was the general idea, Wullie."

"But why?" It was almost a wail. "Who cares in Glasgow at all if there's some kind of sea serpent in Loch Moyne?"

"Mr. Cruikshank does. Simply said, it's just a matter of cold cash. Come to think of it, it doesn't have to be cold, either. The more visitors to Loch Moyne, the more business for Mr. Cruikshank and some others. I can't really blame them too much." He tapped the stem of his pipe reflectively against his teeth. "Just the same, Wullie, I'm afraid that your shy little friend Maggie has just about seen the last of the peace and quiet she has always known in Loch Moyne. Unless I miss my guess, when the sensational stories and pictures of the Loch Moyne Monster get around the country, Abermuir will suddenly be on the map. And with Abermuir on the map, the tourists will be on the road. By the thousands. And all roads leading here."

"Aye," was all Wullie could say. He felt sick at heart for Maggie and her only wanting to be left alone in the solitude of Loch Moyne. He felt sick at heart too for Ian Grant. Only now was he beginning to realize what he had done when he had foolishly gone to Hector Cruikshank. For no matter how the story was handled in the press, the young professor was sure to find his name in the headlines. After all, it had been he, Ian Grant, Assistant Professor of Paleontology at the University of Glasgow, who had seen the strange creature in the loch and had taken the picture. He too had been the one who had identified the sea monster as a plesiosaur, although the identification had been a tentative one, pending consultation with his fellow scientists. But Mr. Cruikshank had struck first. And the proprietor of Ye Olde Village Tea Shoppe was hardly concerned with the niceties of scientific investigation. His story would be short and to the point. There was a prehistoric monster in Loch Moyne. And he had a photograph of it to prove it—a photograph taken by a professor from one of the leading universities.

In a way, Wullie reflected sadly, Maggie and Professor Grant had much in common. They both had wanted to be left alone, to go about their own business in their own way. All of that was impossible now. And it was he, Wullie Watson, who had spoiled everything for both of them. That Ian Grant had been so nice about it too had, in a way, only added to Wullie's bitterness at what he had done. It only reminded him the more how selfish had been his own act in contrast to the generous behavior of the visitor.

Ian Grant ran his fingers through Wullie's spiky hair. "Cheer up! It's not that bad. The news was bound to get around anyway. Furthermore I can always explain to the reporters, if I have to, that Maggie's not a real monster. Or at any rate she's not a fifty-foot monster. Actually, if she is a genuine plesiosaur, and I think she is, then she is what we would call today a living fossil. That is the term first given by Charles Darwin to any animal or plant that has survived its era. That's really all your little friend is—if she's what I think she is. A living fossil." He paused and a slight grimace crossed his face. "There's just one thing, Wullie."

The boy raised his head. "And what will that be, Professor Grant?"

70

The Smallest Monster in the World

"I'm afraid the newspapers are a lot more interested in monsters than they are in fossils."

Professor Grant had been right. The first newspaper to reach Abermuir the next day had the story splashed all over the front page. That is, what was left of the front page, for most if it was taken up by a picture of a gigantic creature that Wullie could scarcely believe was the timid little Maggie he had seen in Loch Moyne. Under the artful hand of Hector Cruikshank every feature had been magnified and somehow subtly altered. The row of small, conical teeth was now a picket fence of sharp daggers. The tiny flippers by which Maggie propelled herself through the water now seemed to resemble nothing more than four monstrous talons, poised to strike. And as Maggie's neck took up half of Maggie, it took up half of Mr. Cruikshank's picture, although somehow it seemed longer. One almost expected to see smoke billowing out from the dragon-like nostrils. Furthermore, all of the background had been carefully cropped out by the wily Mr. Cruikshank so that all one could see was some huge creature, with fangs bared, churning through the water.

"But that's not Maggie!" Wullie cried in dismay as he stared at the newspaper Fiona had just come home with. "It's—it's a monster!"

Fiona nodded, sober-faced. Gone was the good-natured air of superiority she normally affected when her small brother was around. Her lips were set and tight and Wullie noticed there were worried lines around her eyes. He was grateful—if a little surprised—at her concern. Aye, and after the way she had laughed about Maggie! It just went to show how wrong you could be about people. Even sisters.

"I don't like it, Wullie," she said. "Just look at this headline. *Monster Discovered in Small Scottish Loch.* And what a sensational story! All about how a Professor Ian Grant identified it as a plesiosaur, a prehistoric sea serpent that grew to a length of fifty feet." She shook her head. "Poor Ian."

"Eh?" exclaimed Wullie, somewhat startled. "Ian?"

"I mean Professor Grant. You see, Wullie, anyone reading this story is sure to think that what you and Professor Grant saw in the loch was some enormous creature at least fifty feet long. Besides, Ian never stated flatly that it was a plesiosaur. He wanted other scientific opinion. That's why he was in touch with Dr. Smithers in London. Only it's all too late now."

"But isn't there anything we can do at all?" Wullie pleaded.

"I'm afraid not. The whole country knows about it now. They even mentioned it on the radio this morning. In fact there's been so much talk that Mr. Cruikshank suddenly thought the Town Council should call a special meeting for tomorrow night. He thinks Abermuir is sleeping, that it isn't taking advantage of the golden opportunity to make lots of money, now that we're famous." She made a face. "I don't know about Abermuir but I'll tell you somebody who isn't sleeping when there's a chance to make money. Hector Cruikshank."

"You mean he's going to sell lots of tea?"

"Lots and lots of tea, Wullie, to lots and lots of tourists." She smiled thinly and tossed the newspaper onto the sofa.

Wullie looked perplexed. "But I'm not understanding at all. Suppose the visitors show up but Maggie doesn't? After all, she's a shy one. I'm thinking she's not likely to poke her head up if she knows she's going to be stared at. And if she doesn't show up and the visitors get angry and leave, what happens then?"

Fiona's eyes were bleak. "I don't know, Wullie," she said softly. "Only—" She stopped and looked out of the window at Glen Duran, shrouded in a fine, wet mist.

"Only what, Fiona?"

"Only I wouldn't want to be Ian Grant."

The Town Hall was packed the following night

when Sandy Jamison, the Lord Provost of Abermuir, called the meeting to order. No one, not even Fergus MacPhee, who was eighty-eight and the oldest man in all of Glen Duran, could remember ever having seen so many of his neighbors in the same place at the same time. It was quite clear why they were there. All of a sudden Abermuir was News. For more than three hundred years the little village had drowsed at the head of the loch, unnoticed by the outside world, and taken for granted by the local crofters and fishermen. But that had been yesterday. Everything was different today. It would always be different now that some queer type of prehistoric monster had been found in Loch Moyne.

Wullie squeezed into a narrow seat between his father and Fiona at the back of the hall. He craned his neck. Everyone in the village seemed to be there; everyone, that is, except Ian Grant. Wullie experienced a sharp twinge of disappointment when he realized that the professor would not be there. Only then did he remember that Fiona had said just yesterday that he had been called suddenly to London for consultations and would be gone for some time. Funny thing how lately Fiona seemed to know an awful lot about the professor and his plans, almost as though he confided in her. This was daft when you thought about it, her being a girl besides.

The Smallest Monster in the World

The members of the Town Council sat in a half circle on a raised platform, facing the villagers. There was a microphone in front of Sandy Jamison, the Lord Provost. The faces of most of the council members were properly solemn, befitting both the occasion and their own position in the community. Sandy Jamison, a meek little man with thick glasses and nervous gestures, appeared awed by the size of the crowd and the surge of recent events. He seemed to breathe a sigh of relief when, after a few halting and rambling remarks, he turned the meeting over to his fellow council member, Hector Cruikshank.

There was nothing halting or rambling about the proprietor of Ye Olde Village Tea Shoppe as he took the microphone and faced the suddenly tense and expectant audience.

"My friends, I will not waste any words. You are all aware of the momentous revelations of the past few days. Right here in our own Loch Moyne a discovery has been made that has shaken the scientific world to its very foundations!" Mr. Cruikshank's voice trembled with emotion. "I do not doubt, my friends, but at this very moment—at this very moment, mind you—scientists everywhere, in London, in New York, in Moscow, are gathered in hushed assembly to discuss the extraordinary happening of the last few days: that in a small Scottish loch a

75

strange creature has been found, the like of which has not been seen for a hundred million years!"

There was a quick stir in the crowd and an intaking of breaths as the villagers, swept along by the dramatic flow of words, waited for the speaker to continue.

"I had hoped, my friends, that Professor Grant who identified the creature as a plesiosaur, a type of sea monster growing to a length of fifty feet, I had hoped that he would be here in person this evening. Unfortunately Professor Grant had to leave for certain scientific consultations in London. I know he is thinking of us on this historic occasion." Hector Cruikshank took a sip of water from the glass on the lectern.

"Oh, the lying man!" Fiona whispered fiercely, her green eyes blazing. "He just found out yesterday that Ian was going to London. That's why all of a sudden he called this meeting for tonight. He didn't want Ian here!"

"I need hardly tell you," Hector Cruikshank continued, "what all of this will mean to our village. It will mean first of all that we can no longer go about our affairs as we have in the past. It will mean that in the next few days a human tide of scholars, of tourists, of curiosity seekers will be flooding into the countryside around Loch Moyne. These people will have to be housed. They will have to be fed. Their cars will have to be serviced and parked. Many of them will be looking for souvenirs to take home." He paused and raised his beefy arm theatrically over his head. "Abermuir must be ready to accept the challenge of history! Abermuir cannot let these people down. Abermuir will not let them down. We must rise to meet our destiny! We must work, all of us, so that when the world at large thinks of Abermuir it will instantly think of monsters."

Sandy Jamison, the Lord Provost, squirmed uneasily in his chair. Twice he opened his mouth to say something but each time he caught Hector Cruikshank's cold eyes and hastily swallowed whatever words he was going say.

"Last night the idea occurred to me that we should formally change the name of our village from Abermuir to Monsterville. We could have had a banner across High Street with the message 'Welcome to Monsterville—Where the Monsters Make their Home!'" He frowned. "On second thought I realized that some of our jealous neighbors might purposely misread the message. Reluctantly I decided we should keep the name of our village as it is."

The Lord Provost finally found his voice. "Monsterville? But Mr. Cruikshank, that would mean that

I would be the Lord Provost of Monsterville!" He looked distressed and wrung his hands. "I mean, I appreciate the honor—"

"We are not changing the name," Hector Cruikshank interrupted impatiently with a wave of his arm. "But we are, I hope, changing our attitude. Abermuir, like it or not, has moved into the twentieth century. Just like our monster in the loch. And if we're going to do justice to the monster, we have to be monster-minded. We have to think monster. We have to let the whole world know not only that Abermuir has a monster but that we're proud of it!" His eyes twinkled. "And if it means a few honest shillings for all of us, then fine I say!"

"And fine I say too!" Rab Douglas cried out, his face flushed with excitement. Rab Douglas was the village baker. "You're right, Hector! Abermuir's been asleep too long! Now that we've got a monster, I say let's put it to work!"

"I'm with you, Rab!" Jack Simpson, the butcher, chimed in. "Somebody will have to feed all the tourists who'll be coming here and it might as well be us!"

"That's right, Jack!" exclaimed Dugal Scott. "It's time Abermuir woke up!" Dugal ran the small tobacco shop across the street from the post office. Dugal, a moody, taciturn man, normally gave out small talk as begrudgingly as he gave out change. Only this was a different Dugal Scott, a Dugal Scott fired by the vision that Hector Cruikshank had cleverly painted. A vision of "a few honest shillings" —then a few more and a few more after that as the tourists poured into Abermuir, their money restless in their well-lined pockets.

A chorus of agreement rose from around the crowded hall as the rest of the villagers caught the fever. Only a few seemed remote from the mass excitement. Sandy Jamison, the Lord Provost, looked both glum and uneasy on the platform. Fergus Mac-Phee, the oldest man in the village, on the other hand, seemed bored. Fergus sat, slumped forward in his chair, his eyes watery and half closed, a gentle smile on his lips when Hector Cruikshank finally gave up the microphone. The gentle smile was still on his face as a dozen villagers leaped to their feet after Mr. Cruikshank had stepped down, all of them urging resolutions on how Abermuir should best exploit the monster. When the meeting broke up an hour later the Town Council had passed a sweeping series of motions. One of them called for the purchase of a number of giant balloons, shaped and colored to resemble monsters. Moored to the village green by long ropes, the helium filled blimps would float over Abermuir, visible for miles. Another resolution set up a committee, with Hector Cruikshank as chairman, to develop new ideas on how to promote Abermuir as an all year tourist attraction. The final motion passed by the council authorized a series of advertisements to be placed in the city newspapers calling attention to the recent sensational happenings in Loch Moyne and listing the accommodations available in Abermuir.

"Quite a meeting," Mr. Watson said later that evening as he leaned back in his big armchair by the fire. "I can't say I'm one of Hector Cruikshank's warmest admirers but still you have to give the man credit. He really knows how to sell his ideas."

Mrs. Watson sniffed. "And himself. Not forgetting Ye Olde Village Tea Shoppe. What I didn't like was the way the whole community went along with him. Nobody seemed to care at all what happened to Abermuir as long as everybody made money."

"What I didn't like," Fiona added, a slight edge biting her voice, "was the sly way that Hector Cruikshank made it appear that the creature in the loch which Professor Grant had identified was fifty feet long." Her eyes flashed with indignation. "Ian asked me just before he left to wait until he got back from London before saying anything to anyone. It's a good thing he did. I would have given Mr. Hector Cruikshank a nice piece of my mind! Yes, and that

bit about changing the name of the village to Monsterville. If you ask me, the real monster around
here isn't in the loch. It's in Ye Olde Village Tea
Shoppe!"

"Now, now Fiona," her father reproved, "that's
not quite fair. In wanting to capitalize on the monster, Hector isn't a great deal different from a lot of
others—Rab Douglas, Jack Simpson, Dugal Scott, to
name just a few. Where he does differ, however, is
in his ability to plan and to get things done." He
paused. "What really convinced me was something
I heard after the meeting tonight while I was speaking to Sandy Jamison. It proved, if nothing else did,
that Hector Cruikshank knows how to get Abermuir
on the map."

Wullie looked at his father curiously. "Something
you heard? Tonight?"

Gavin Watson hesitated for a moment, then
shrugged. "The news is bound to be out tomorrow
morning anyhow. A TV crew from London is coming up to Abermuir next Saturday."

Wullie stared. "And why now should they be
thinking of doing that?"

"Why? To take pictures of course."

"Pictures of what?" Wullie asked.

"Of the monster," Gavin Watson replied. He
reached for his pipe.

CHAPTER NINE

TAKE pictures of Maggie?" Wullie repeated dully.
"That's right," Gavin Watson said. He
tapped tobacco into the bowl of his pipe. "Just
think. No one ever visits Loch Moyne. Or hardly
ever. Yet next week up to fifty million people are
going to be dropping in. Figuratively, that is, Wullie.
All of them will be peering over the shoulder of the
camera, hoping for a glimpse of the monster that
has set the whole country talking, thanks to our
enterprising Hector Cruikshank."

"Fifty million people?" was all Wullie could say.

"If they all watch. And in addition to those in
front of their TV sets, thousands more will be flock-
ing here to see the monster in person. They will be

streaming into Abermuir by bus and car from all over Scotland and England." He grinned at his solemn-eyed son. "Maybe no one has seen a plesiosaur for a hundred million years but it certainly looks as though a lot of people are going to see this one." He paused. "If it shows up."

"She won't show up," Wullie said flatly. "I know she won't." He nibbled at the corner of an oatcake.

Gavin Watson looked with interest at his son. "And why are you so sure she won't?"

"Because Maggie's a shy one. Mr. Peebles told me, and he knows Maggie better than anyone. If Maggie knows there's going to be fifty million people staring at her, she'll never show up."

"Mr. Peebles? And who is Mr. Peebles?"

"A kelpie," exclaimed Wullie. "He lives in the small pool at the end of the burn."

Mr. Watson sighed and half closed his eyes. "Wullie, would you please stop this everlasting daydreaming of yours? There's no such thing as a kelpie and it's time you realized it!" He reached over and picked up a book. "Anyway, for Professor Grant's sake, if for no one else's, I hope this Maggie of yours does show up."

"Professor Grant?" Nan Watson inquired. "What do you mean?"

"Just that he was the one who tentatively identi-

fied the creature that he and Wullie saw as a plesiosaur. He was the one too, who took the picture of it,
regardless of what Hector Cruikshank did to the
picture before he sent it to the newspapers. If he
wasn't a paleontologist it wouldn't matter. But he is.
I'm sure when he comes back from London he'll
have a lot more to say about Mr. Cruikshank and
the story he sent out. But until then a number of
people are going to be awfully unhappy with young
Mr. Grant if the monster doesn't show up next
Saturday."

"But it's not fair, dad," Fiona exclaimed. "I mean
it's perfectly ridiculous to expect some monster to
come leaping out of a Highland loch on cue!"

"That's true, Fiona. But you understand how this
type of program is handled. For example, they may
take you to some old castle which has a legend of
being haunted. The telecast would be set for mid-
night which for some reason is the favorite hour for
ghost-walking. Whether or not one believes in ghosts,
the fact remains that everyone sits on the edge of his
chair secretly hoping that some phantom spirit will
appear. It will be the same sort of show next Saturday, only this time the same people will be waiting
and praying for some grotesque monster to show up.
The only difference is that no one of any scientific
standing ever claimed to have seen a ghost. But we

do have, in the case of the Loch Moyne Monster, an individual who is recognized as an authority in his field and who has, whether intentionally or not, given the story a certain scientific credence. I'm speaking of young Professor Grant."

Wullie heard the voices around him as his mother joined the discussion. His own thoughts were elsewhere. And they were bitter thoughts. It was all his fault. He knew it. If he hadn't talked Professor Grant into going down to the loch that first day the whole business would never have happened. There would have been no picture of Maggie. Even then, everything would have still been all right if he hadn't gone to Mr. Cruikshank and told him the story. That was when everything had really started to happen! Och, and why had he been so daft as to have spoken to the man at all? Couldn't he have known that Mr. Cruikshank was not the type to keep the story in Abermuir?

He wished desperately there was something he could do. Only there was nothing. Nothing anyone could do. Maybe if he prayed it might help.

He stared blankly into the fireplace. The flames rose and fell in a rhythmic dance, like gaily colored puppets dangling from somewhere up the chimney. If only there was something he could do to help Professor Grant. Someone he could turn to. His heart ached with remorse and a thousand agonizing thoughts filled his mind. Och, and if he had just kept his mouth shut! Right from the beginning. Right from the time he had felt so clever and tried to trick Mr. Peebles into having the monster appear—

He stiffened. Mr. Peebles! Of course! Why had he not thought of him sooner? Maggie had listened to him before. She would listen again.

And the day would be saved for Professor Grant.

The small seamed face of the kelpie screwed itself up into a frown. "Television? Are you sure that's what it's called? I've never heard of it."

"It's an invention," Wullie explained. "You see things that aren't really there."

"If that's all it does," Mr. Peebles said with a fine sneer, "I don't think it was worth inventing in the first place." He sat down on the small flat stone between the two white hawthorn bushes. It was apparently his favorite resting place, for Wullie remembered having seen him at ease there on his earlier visits. The kelpie brushed some thistledown from his green jacket and looked away from the boy. "What is it that you want of me, Wullie Watson?"

"A favor."

"A favor is it?" grunted the cross little man. "Yet it is no favor I can give you until I first repay you

86

for getting me out from under that branch. It is not our way to remain beholden to any human."

"Then maybe, Mr. Peebles, you can help me," Wullie cried eagerly. "I was hoping you could ask Maggie to be there on Saturday for the television. Because if she's not there an awful lot of people are going to be angry with Professor Grant and him having nothing to do with it altogether."

"Maggie? But Maggie would never do it," Mr. Peebles snapped. "You know how she hates crowds. Just the idea of all those people staring at her would drive her out of her wits. Forget it, Wullie Watson!"

"But I can't," the boy returned miserably. "Couldn't you at least ask her?"

"I tell you it wouldn't do any good! Once a plesiosaur makes up its mind, there's no changing it. Besides Maggie is a woman. You know how they are." Mr. Peebles shook his head, causing the green feather in his Robin Hood cap to sway vigorously. "A female plesiosaur can be terribly stubborn."

"So there's nothing at all you can do?" Wullie asked, reluctant to give up the fight.

"Nothing! You got yourself into this mess, boy. Now it's up to you to get yourself out."

"But it's poor Professor Grant who's in the mess, not me," Wullie explained. "And it wasn't his fault at all. It was mine."

"Your fault?" Mr. Peebles darted a quick suspicious look at the boy.

"Aye."

"Not his?"

Wullie shook his head.

"Hm. First time I ever heard of one human wanting to help another." He scowled. "I hate to say this, Wullie Watson, but I like you. Still I don't know what I can do to help. The moment I tell Maggie what's waiting for her above water, I know what her answer is going to be." He shook his head decisively. "It's no use."

Wullie said carefully, "But supposing you didn't tell her, Mr. Peebles?"

"Eh? Didn't tell her what?"

"That there was anyone waiting for her? Supposing now you just asked her to show up? Fine I'm knowing she would do it if you only asked her."

"You mean not tell her about all the people waiting for her on the surface?" Mr. Peebles looked kind of startled.

"Aye."

"Hm. And how many people did you say would be watching on this television thing?"

"Fifty million."

The kelpie shuddered. "Fifty million? She's always kept pretty much to herself, has Maggie."

"But she will not be knowing at all that they're watching, Mr. Peebles. All she'll see will be the people around Loch Moyne."

"That should be a big comfort," Mr. Peebles returned tartly. "And remember, Maggie, like all plesiosaurs, has three eyes in her head. There's not much escapes her." He gnawed on a knuckle thoughtfully. "Still, it's an idea, Wullie Watson," he conceded grudgingly. "What time did you say on Saturday?"

"Three o'clock, Mr. Peebles!" Wullie replied joyfully. "Och now and I can't thank you enough!"

"I know you can't," the little man snapped. "So don't bother trying. I just hope I'm not making a mistake. I wouldn't be doing this at all if I wasn't beholden to you."

"You have the good heart," Wullie said. All of a sudden his own felt as light as thistledown.

"And the soft head," Mr. Peebles retorted sourly.

"Three o'clock," Wullie called over his shoulder as he dashed off, "and don't forget to tell Maggie!"

"I'll tell her," Mr. Peebles said crossly. "I'd just like to know what she's going to tell me after this whole business is over with!"

CHAPTER TEN

I N all his life Wullie had never seen such excitement as that which gripped Abermuir in the days
that followed. For that matter neither had Fergus
MacPhee, and he was the oldest man in the village.
From every point of the compass, reporters, scientists, and just plain sightseers came pouring into
Abermuir. High Street, the narrow, cobbled thor-
oughfare which ran the length of the village, got so
jammed with cars and buses at one point that traffic
came to a complete standstill. The entire Abermuir
Police Force in the portly form of Constable Mur-
doch MacVinish did a Herculean job of untangling
the mess, but Wullie noticed that the constable
seemed exhausted and ill-humored after the traffic

was finally moving again. Quite clearly having a monster as an attraction was not going to be an unmixed blessing.

It was shortly after that, that the convoy of trucks arrived bearing the giant balloons which would soon be inflated with lighter-than-air gas and sent soaring over the village. Although there had been lots of technicians in white overalls to arrange for the unloading and setting up of the balloons, Hector Cruikshank had insisted on taking charge. He was everywhere, a carnation in his lapel to signify his status, waving his hands importantly and indicating the mooring points for the ropes. Wullie, in common with everyone else in Abermuir, had gawked as the enormous balloons gently drifted upwards. Long tails twitching, evil teeth bared, they had looked like an army of bloodthirsty dragons tensed to pounce on the defenseless village below.

Hector Cruikshank had no sooner taken care of his airborne monsters than he was off to supervise the erection of a series of billboards overlooking the new macadam highway some miles distant from the village. No motorist could hope to pass without being reminded in letters one foot high that he was approaching Abermuir, home of the Loch Moyne Monster. That job done, he was off to preside at a reception in his tea room for the members of the visiting press. It was remarkable in a way, how many receptions seemed to wind up at Ye Olde Village Tea Shoppe. Business had never been so good.

As the days drew nearer for the telecast, the fever mounted in the village. From time to time groups of visitors would wend their way to the lake, hoping to catch a glimpse of the fearsome Loch Moyne Monster. Yet stare as they might, no dark form ever shattered the glassy surface of the water. Not until the day before the television spectacular did any monster show up on the loch, and that was when one of Hector Cruikshank's balloons snapped its halter and finally came to rest in the loch. Drifting gently in the water, its scales flashing in the sun, its grotesque head swaying with the motion of the water, it set up a field day for the grinning photographers and seemed to heighten the carnival spirit of the crowd. Perhaps too the amused spectators saw in the incident of the artificial monster in the loch, a good augury for the appearance of the real one the following day.

In a way, when one thought about it, as Wullie did often, it was strange that anyone should really expect that the monster would show up promptly at three o'clock Saturday afternoon, simply because the television cameras would be waiting for her. He was sure that, if pressed, the lighthearted visitors in their gay holiday attire would have agreed. It just didn't make any sense at all. Yet there it was. And sense or not, everyone went on treating the affair as a sort of TV Special Events program, with the monster scheduled to go into its act right after the commercial. After all, if television could push around cabinet ministers and cricket players, it could jolly well push around a plesiosaur. It all came with the price of the set.

Abermuir came to a complete halt the following afternoon as the villagers made their way down to the loch. Only Hector Cruikshank and Fergus MacPhee remained behind, the proprietor of Ye Olde Village Tea Shoppe because he was too busy adding up his receipts and replenishing his depleted stock of cakes and scones, and Old Fergus, because he opined that there were enough monsters loose in the world already and he saw no reason to limp all the way down to Loch Moyne, with his arthritis, to see another one.

Wullie stood with Fiona and their father and mother on a small plateau of sparse yellow grass and huddling clumps of heather. The spot was just above and to the right of Lamont Castle and offered a fine panorama of the entire loch. A television camera had been set up on the narrow promontory from where the professor and Wullie had first seen Maggie. Another camera, like a one-eyed Cyclops,

The Smallest Monster in the World

stared fixedly at Loch Moyne from high up on the mountain on the other side of the water. Parked nearby was a specially equipped truck with a generator and a complete control-room setup. A group of technicians—an audio engineer, a switcher, a camera control man and a director—made last-minute adjustments and occasionally glanced at their watches. Everything was in readiness for the monster.

As Wullie watched the preparation and the stillness that seemed to be settling on the crowd, a growing uneasiness claimed him. Supposing nothing happened? Supposing Mr. Peebles forgot to tell Maggie? Or supposing Maggie simply refused to go along with the idea? After all, Maggie was a woman and a shy one besides. If she didn't show up there could be trouble. The massed spectators expected something to happen. That was why they had come to Abermuir in the first place. They would feel that in some way they had been cheated, although exactly why they should feel so would have been difficult to explain.

"Five minutes," Fiona said looking down at her watch. There was a troubled look in her eyes. Apparently she too did not like the look of things.

"That's right, Fiona, five minutes," a familiar voice sang out from just behind them. "Thought

I'd never find you people! There was no one in the village when I got there but old Fergus MacPhee and a mob of airborne monsters! Gave me quite a fright, I tell you."

"Professor Grant!" Wullie cried out joyfully as he spun around and recognized the speaker. "Och, and are we glad to see you!"

Ian Grant smiled broadly as he shook hands all around. Wullie noticed that it took him longer to shake hands with Fiona than anyone else. In fact he never did quite get his hand back.

"No more glad than I am to see you folks! Thought I'd never get out of London. All of the questions they kept firing at me about Maggie! They were most understanding and helpful, though, and tremendously excited. An official statement is going to be released in a couple of days."

Fiona said, "We missed you, Ian. It's been lonely around here without you."

"Eh? Lonely?" The young professor affected an expression of bewilderment as he gazed around him. "Never saw so many people in one place at the same time."

"The wrong people," Fiona said. "Besides I'm just beginning to learn that the bigger the crowd the more lonely you can feel. Crazy, isn't it?"

Ian grinned slightly. "That's odd. I noticed that

too while I was in London. Never was so lonely in my life." He let his eyes travel with cynical amusement over the massed spectators. "Are they kidding? Do they really think that somebody on television presses little buttons and *presto!* strange creatures pop up from subterranean depths?"

Mr. Watson smiled. "I agree with you, Ian. The whole thing is ridiculous. Why should any marine creature show up just to please a television audience? Yet although I know it's ridiculous I'm here just the same, so I'm no better than anyone else. Psychologists have glib explanations for mass behavior which contradict reason. Perhaps deep down inside we believe there's something in this business of wish fulfillment. Especially when that wish is emotionally heightened by sharing it with others."

Ian Grant nodded thoughtfully. "Just think! Out there behind these cameras are fifty million pairs of eyes, all fixed on this little body of water that we call Loch Moyne. The brains behind each of these pairs of eyes will be pleading for something to emerge from the depths of the loch. We know very little about the power—if any—of such tremendous concentrations of massed wills." He shrugged. "That said, I'm willing to bet ten shillings to a sixpence our friend Maggie stays home."

Wullie shook his head stubbornly. "She'll be here, sir. I know she will."

"Three o'clock," Fiona observed. There was an edge of forced lightheartedness to her voice but the green eyes focused on the loch were thoughtful, wondering.

The murmur of voices hushed away into a silence deeper than the loch itself. In the sudden stillness a solitary curlew drifted across the sky, its bittersweet cry trailing behind it like a melodious kite. Slowly the minutes ticked away. It was four minutes past three. Five. Six. Nothing stirred in the loch. Hardly a ripple disturbed the glass-smooth surface.

A restive murmur, a few sheepish laughs had just started to rise from the crowd when suddenly, just off the promontory by Lamont Castle, a small, flat wrinkle appeared in the water. The next moment, as the massed spectators gaped, the small flat wrinkle became a small flat head. It was followed immediately by a slender snakelike neck and a squat body with flippers on each side. For almost ten seconds the strange creature remained motionless on the surface. Then after a nervous, corkscrew turn of the head, the body started to slip back into the loch. Slowly the water lapped up the length of the neck as the creature sank down deeper. Finally only a small head remained on top, a small head with nostrils high on the skull and three unblinking eyes. Then it too was gone. Except for a few widening circles in the water off Lamont Castle, nothing stirred on the surface of Loch Moyne.

"Good-by, Maggie," Wullie whispered. Somehow he was certain, deep in his heart, that never again would he see Maggie, the smallest monster in the world.

As though awakened from a spell, a slow rumble started to rise from the crowd as it realized that nothing more was going to happen.

"Was that the monster?" a red-faced man demanded.

"It's a fraud!" screamed a high-pitched voice charged with anger. "Just look at the size of these balloons they've got over Abermuir! They could make fifty of what we just saw!"

A heavy-set man standing near Ian Grant waved his umbrella furiously at the loch. "And I came all the way from Glasgow to see that! Why I've seen bigger monsters running around Sauchiehall Street on leashes!"

"We've been tricked!" bellowed a small, fat man at the top of his lungs. "And I know who did the tricking. It was that crook, Cruikshank! He's the one who put up all those phony balloons!"

"Aye," growled a rough voice from just behind

Wullie, "and another thing he put up was the price of his rotten tea. I've been paying a shilling a cup to that robber and I just found out that last week he couldn't get eightpence! Well, I'm getting my money back!"

"And I'm jolly well getting mine!"

"Me too!"

Amid a chorus of incensed voices the crowd took off in the direction of Ye Olde Village Tea Shoppe. Ian Grant scratched his head and looked after the irate figures, an expression of whimsical concern on his face.

"Hope they don't do anything drastic to Mr. Cruikshank," he murmured. "He's really not such a bad sort. Just has a thing about million-year-old monsters."

"He had," Mr. Watson returned drily. He watched, bemused, as the long column of indignant visitors surged towards the tea room. "Somehow I have the feeling that after today Hector Cruikshank will be quite content to wait another million years before seeing his next one."

CHAPTER ELEVEN

W HEN the last of the disgruntled visitors shook
the dust of Abermuir from his feet, the entire
village breathed a long, slow sigh of relief. Now that
it was all over Abermuir was happy that it had
turned out just the way it had. If there was to be
any monster in Loch Moyne everyone was quite content that it be the smallest one in the world. Big
monsters meant big crowds. And big crowds in
turn meant noise and traffic and bad tempers. Even
Hector Cruikshank—a somewhat chastened Hector
Cruikshank after the damage his tea room had
suffered at the hands of the irate visitors—even he
had made no protest when the last of the great balloons was put away. As a matter of fact, he had even

lent a hand in the deflation, plainly relieved to have things in Abermuir the way they had always been.

It took only a few weeks for the world to forget all about Abermuir. There were other things to think about. A new moon shot. A new crisis in the Middle East. A new singing combo from Liverpool which had startled the pop world by appearing in the most extreme and daring of male hair styles yet—military crew cuts. Only a few scholars continued to discuss the strange thing which had recently taken place in a remote village in the Scottish Highlands.

If the world was quick in forgetting, so too was Abermuir. True, once in a while the subject of the monster came up and the villagers would laugh a little shamefacedly as they remembered how they had behaved at the time of the incident. When all was said and done no one had really made any money out of the business. Still, in another sense, each of the villagers had profited in some way from the experience. For he knew now, as he may not have known before, that the true riches of this world come in many guises—the contentment when one shares an open fire with friends; the peace that stretches the heart at eventide when the world is still and the only sound is the soft slap of loch water against smooth white pebbles.

Of all the unexpected things that happened following Maggie's brief debut on television, none was more unexpected to Wullie than that Ian Grant should ask Fiona to marry him. Wullie had been too stunned to talk when he first learned of it which, for Wullie, was being pretty stunned indeed. Och, and the man must have taken leave of his senses entirely! Fiona of all people! Only later was he able to come up with an answer that partly satisfied him. Professor Grant was a paleontologist. The older a thing became, the more curious he was about it. Fiona was getting on in years. Nineteen. It would make sense that the more ancient she became the more interesting she would become to him. Wullie nodded to himself, somewhat reassured. It was queer just the same how a man could get himself so wrapped up in his work!

With Ian Grant busy with the preparations for the new school year and the wedding, Wullie had little chance to talk over with him the events of the past few weeks. It was no sense, of course, talking to Fiona. Ever since her engagement she had been in another world, a world that severely excluded small brothers named Wullie. As for his mother and father, they just nodded absently and said, "Yes, Wullie," whenever he mentioned Maggie. Obviously the subject was no longer of interest to them. Just as it was no longer of interest to anyone else in Abermuir

Except Wullie. Often, when he was by himself he found his thoughts turning to the little monster, the smallest monster in the world, just as they turned on a certain morning four weeks later as he sat, his chin cupped between his clasped hands and stared down at Loch Moyne. Och, and she must have been the frightened wee thing indeed, he mused, when she had looked around that day and spied the masses of people goggling at her! And she such a shy one besides! It had taken a special kind of courage not to flee right away. But Maggie had gone gracefully, like the lady she was.

Wullie frowned. It wasn't right somehow that she would never know how grateful he was for everything she had done. Yet how could he thank her if he never saw her again? Suddenly he sat up straight. Of course! Mr. Peebles! He would tell him, and Maggie would learn from the kelpie that someone appreciated what she had done.

Mr. Peebles! As Wullie leaped to his feet and started running he was surprised to remember that he hadn't seen the cantankerous little kelpie since just before the great telecast. As a matter of fact he had celebrated his ninth birthday since he had last spoken to Mr. Peebles. Strange how in the rush of events he had forgotten all about the kelpie who lived in the pool at the end of the burn. He smiled to himself as he saw again in his mind's eye the little figure in the green coat sitting in his accustomed place between the two hawthorn bushes.

He halted, scarcely breathing fast, when he reached the pool. He glanced around. "Mr. Peebles!" he called. "Mr. Peebles!"

There was no answer.

He crossed over to the small flat stone between the two bushes. There was no one there.

"Mr. Peebles!" Wullie cried again, only a little louder this time. "It's me—Wullie Watson!"

Again there was no answer. The boy hesitated, not quite certain what to do next. Mr. Peebles had always been there before. Wullie parted a few lacy bracken fronds and peered behind them. It was unlike Mr. Peebles to play games. Still, one could never tell about kelpies. "Mr. Peebles!" he called. He waited, his ears alert for the familiar scolding voice. The only sound was the slow hum of a bee drowsing among the clover.

The boy bit his lip. He made his way to the edge of the pool. After all, Mr. Peebles was a water kelpie. If he was anywhere he would be in the pool where he normally lived. "Mr. Peebles!" he cried, staring down into the water. "Are you there, Mr. Peebles?" There was no movement in the pool.

He was just on the point of calling again when he

heard a slight movement from somewhere behind him. He swung around. His eyes opened wide with astonishment when he recognized the bent figure making its way slowly towards him. It was Fergus MacPhee, the oldest man in Abermuir.

"Well now, Mr. MacPhee, and I was hardly expecting to see you here at all," the boy exclaimed.

Fergus did not answer. His breathing came slowly, audibly. Although the day was warm he had on the long black coat he always wore. He dug deep into one of the pockets and produced a grimy handkerchief. He dabbed at the beads of sweat that glistened on the loose skin around his throat. Finally, with a soft sigh of relief he eased himself down on the trunk of a fallen tree.

"I thought someone was drowning, Wullie Watson! Never heard the like of all that yelling that was going on! I'm thinking they could have heard you all the way down in Abermuir."

Wullie smiled. He liked Old Fergus. Who in the village did not? He was a gentle, placid soul who bothered no one, a familiar figure in his faded black coat, his white hair streaming over his shoulders. Fergus MacPhee had never married and since the death of his younger sister, Annie, had lived by himself in the small croft his father had left him on the edge of Glen Duran.

"I was looking for Mr. Peebles," Wullie explained, before he remembered that Old Fergus could scarcely know who Mr. Peebles was.

"Ah yes, Mr. Peebles." Fergus MacPhee nodded his head in agreement. He fished in another pocket of his black coat and came up with a small square of cheese which he popped into his mouth. "Mr. Peebles, of course."

Wullie stared at him in astonishment. "You will be knowing him then?"

"I do that."

Wullie looked doubtful. "Mr. Peebles is a kelpie," he explained carefully.

Fergus smiled. "Well now and I'd be surprised if he was anything else and the same one only five inches from the tip of his toes to the crown of his head." He paused. "And what for will you be after wanting Mr. Peebles?"

"He did a favor for me. He and somebody else. Somebody called Maggie. Mr. Peebles knows her. I wanted him to tell her I'm grateful."

"So tell him," Old Fergus said with a shrug as he groped for another piece of cheese.

"Aye, but he's not here at all."

"But of course he is, Wullie Watson! That's him right over there."

"Eh?" Wullie looked around. "Where?"

"Over there! Right where I'm pointing."

Wullie followed the direction of Old Fergus' outstretched finger. There was a small flat rock there, between two white hawthorn bushes. It was the spot where Mr. Peebles usually sat. Only he wasn't there now.

Fergus must have caught the bewilderment on the boy's face, for a look of understanding came into his eyes. "Ah yes. So that will be the way of it, eh lad? You can no longer see our friend Mr. Peebles?"

"But he's not there!" Wullie cried. "There's nothing there between the two bushes! Nothing at all but a flat stone!"

Fergus said softly, "So you are growing up then, Wullie Watson."

Wullie frowned. What on earth was Old Fergus getting at? "I was nine two weeks ago."

"Nine?" The old man nodded absently. "Ah yes. Fine now, I remember. I was nine myself when the kelpie went away. It was seventy years later before I saw him again. Exactly in the same spot by this pool where I had left him. Seventy years, mind you. A long time that. A long time."

Wullie stared. Fergus MacPhee must surely be having fun with him! He said slyly, to trap the old man, "Och now, Mr. MacPhee, as long as you can

see the kelpie sitting over there you won't mind at all telling me how he's dressed?"

Fergus MacPhee shrugged and squinted at the space between the two bushes. "Let me see now. He's wearing a suit of some kind of Lincoln green. And there's a row of mother-of-pearl buttons down the middle. On his wee feet he has brown pointed sandals. And on his head there's a Robin Hood cap with a green feather."

Wullie stood quite still. He stared again at the spot between the two hawthorn bushes. There was nothing there. Nothing at all except a flat stone, a little grass, and a few clumps of heather. Yet Fergus MacPhee had described Mr. Peebles' dress exactly. And in some way he had known that it was here, between the two small bushes that the kelpie usually sat. But how had he known? Quite plainly there was a mystery here, a mystery that teased and troubled the mind.

"Do not be asking me, lad, how such things are," Old Fergus said, "for I'm not certain at all that I'm understanding them myself."

Wullie nodded doubtfully. "Yet it is strange, is it not, Mr. MacPhee, that you will be seeing something over there between these two bushes that I will not be seeing myself?"

Old Fergus hesitated. "I was never a clever one

with the words and some things are not easy in the telling." He paused as though collecting his thoughts and then shook his head and sighed. "Perhaps it is just that there are things we see when we are very young that we lose as we grow older. Aye, perhaps that is the way of it. Only later on, when we are very old, do they come back again. For the things of which I speak, Wullie, are seen not just with the eyes but with the heart and the mind as well."

Wullie said, "Then someday maybe I'll see Mr. Peebles again?"

"Aye, some day. A long day from now though. Meantime you will start to forget all about Mr. Peebles. Or if you remember him at all you'll laugh to yourself quietly and think it was all a queer foolishness and him a kelpie besides. Then one day when you are very old, Wullie, you will come alone to this place. And as you sit here remembering the days of long ago, all of a sudden you will spy a little man peering up at you, a little man with a cross look to him and dressed all in green. And it will be Mr. Peebles."

"Yes." Wullie responded doubtfully. He wanted very much to believe that what Old Fergus had just said was true. Only there was a small doubt in his voice, just as there was a small doubt in his heart. It was strange how already some of the happenings of the past few weeks were beginning to fade in his memory. The outlines were not so sharp in his mind, the colors not so bright. Had there really been a Mr. Peebles? After all, everyone said he dreamed too much. And it had all happened a long time ago—when he was eight. Besides, when you thought about it, Fergus MacPhee sitting over there on that tree trunk, his watery eyes partly closed as he dozed, was an old man. A very old man. Everyone knew that men that old dreamed foolish dreams; sitting forever with their withered faces lifted up to the sun; hearing voices long since muted; seeing faces long since vanished.

Wullie turned his eyes from Old Fergus and stared off into the distance at where Loch Moyne lay splintered with sunlight far below. "A hundred million years," he said, "that's a long time."

The old man looked up with a start. "Eh?"

"I said a hundred million years is a long time, Mr. MacPhee."

Fergus looked questioningly at the boy, then at the glistening surface of the loch, the home of a certain small monster named Maggie. The smallest monster in the world. "It will depend on how one looks at it, Wullie Watson," he said. "Nine years is a long time too."

The boy nodded. Old Fergus was right. Nine years

was a long time. Already it seemed ages since he had been eight and had first met Mr. Peebles. Still it was necessary that he get the last word in. "Just the same, Mr. MacPhee, you'll have to admit yourself that a hundred million years is a long time to spend in one place."

Fergus MacPhee's eyes traveled slowly from the loch to the rock-faced hills; to the brooding corries that once had echoed to the wild hulloos of the clansmen; to the great sweep of Glen Duran in the distance. "Maybe it's just a question of finding the right place."

"Maybe that's it," Wullie said.